Pon-Pon

Sequel to *Day-Day* and the Award-Winning *Chop, Chop*

Book Three

L.N. Cronk

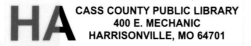

ISBN Number: 978-0-9820027-2-8
Library of Congress Control Number: 2008933273

Published by Rivulet Publishing
West Jefferson, NC, 28694, U.S.A.

Dedicated to the members of my very first book club.

. . . if anyone competes as an athlete, he does not receive the victor's crown unless he competes according to the rules. 2 Timothy 2:5

~ ~ ~

I LOOKED AT his picture before I took it off the wall. Then I pulled it down and looked into Greg's eyes.

"We're going home!" I told him. Just in case you're wondering, I *don't* usually talk to pictures of dead people, but I was particularly excited about moving back to Cavendish and I really wished I could share it with my best friend.

"Did you say something?" Laci asked, sticking her head in the door to my office.

"Nope."

She looked at what I was holding.

"You okay?" she asked.

"I'm great," I said, smiling. "How 'bout you?"

She nodded and tried to smile, but mostly she just nodded. She was nowhere near as excited to be leaving Mexico as I was, but God had let her know what He wanted us to do: He wanted us to go home. Laci always did what God told her to do and I was only too happy to comply.

We'd just finished the paperwork for Lily's adoption and she was all ours. As far as I was concerned, once I got the pictures from my office wall and had my family on a plane back to the United States, I didn't care if I ever set foot in Mexico again.

Lily started crying from the other room.

"Dorito!" Laci called. She looked at me. "He woke her up . . . I know he did. He just can't leave her alone . . . she was sound asleep."

"I didn't do anything!" Dorito called back.

Okay, *technically* his real name is Doroteo, but by now even Laci called him Dorito most of the time. When we'd first met him he'd been a toddler . . . recently abandoned in a nearby park. She'd harped on me for months about how I shouldn't call him Dorito, but a good

1

nickname's hard to shake and eventually she'd given up. We figured by now he was about five years old, but we'd never know for sure.

He was all ours too.

"Are you in Lily's room?" I asked, sticking my head into the hallway and looking toward her room. He poked his head out of her doorway.

"I was just *looking* at her . . . I didn't do anything!"

Lily was still crying. Laci looked at me and sighed wearily.

"I'll get her," I said, leaning Greg's picture against the wall of my office.

"No," she said. "But if you could just please, *please* keep him busy for a little while . . ."

"Come here, Dorito," I said. He trudged down the hall toward me, looking sullenly at Laci as she went in to quiet Lily down. I looked down at him and raised an eyebrow.

"I didn't do anything!" he said again. "All I did was breathe!"

Lily was completely deaf so I doubted if him just breathing would have done it. More than likely he'd been pushing stuffed animals into her crib "for her to play with".

"Why were you breathing in her room?" I asked. "You need to stay out of there when she's sleeping."

"I just wanted to look at her," he mumbled.

"I know you love her and I know you're *really* glad to have a little sister, but you've got to do what Mommy and Daddy tell you . . . okay?"

He nodded at me.

"You wanna help me pack?"

He nodded again.

"Okay," I said. "Put out your fingers."

He spread his little hands and held them up. I tore ten pieces of tape off of the dispenser and put one on each of his fingers.

That should keep him busy for a while.

"No, no, no," I said, immediately having to unstick two pieces of tape. "You've got to leave your hands just like this and don't let the tape touch itself. You've got a very important job here. Every time I need a piece of tape you have to give it to me. Think you can do that?"

"Yep."

"Okay, good boy."

I sat down on the floor and picked Greg's picture up again. I laid it on a sheet of bubble wrap and covered it up. Then I took three pieces of tape off of Dorito's fingers and sealed the bubble wrap.

"Okay," I said. "How many did you have before I started?"

"Ten."

"How many did I take away?"

"Three."

"How many are left?"

He started counting what was left.

"Eight."

"Try again."

More counting.

"Seven."

"Good."

Next I grabbed a picture of Tanner and Mike and me on a snowmobile. I wrapped it up and took three more pieces of tape off of his fingers.

"Okay," I said. "You had seven and I just took away three more. Now how many do you have?"

"Four."

"Right."

One more picture (of me and Greg and Greg's little sister, Charlotte, on the beach in Florida) and three more pieces of tape.

"Okay. Now, you started out with ten and we used three and then three and then three. How many do we have left now?"

"One!"

"Right. See, three's not a factor of ten . . . that's why we have one left over. If we'd used five and five we wouldn't have had any left over because five *is* a factor of ten. Or if we'd used two and two and two and two and two we wouldn't have any left over either because two's also a factor of ten. Now, if we'd started out with only *nine* we wouldn't have had any left over because three's a factor of nine, but we didn't, we started with ten. Got it?"

He nodded at me.

"You want a piece of bubble wrap, don't you?"

He added a grin to his nod.

"Here," I said, handing him some and closing the door to my office. "But you have to stay in here and do it. It sounds like Mommy got your sister back to sleep."

Charlotte called me while we were on our way to the airport.

Charlotte was Greg's little sister and I'd known her almost all of her life. I'd been twelve when the White's had moved to town and she'd been just a toddler. Now she was sixteen years old.

"Hey, Charlotte."

"Mom says we can't come and meet you at the airport."

"Why not?"

"She says everything's going to be too *'overwhelming'* for Dorito and that we need to let you guys get settled in first."

"You tell your mom that Dorito's the most easy going kid she's ever met and that if you two aren't at the airport I'm going to be mad."

"Okay," she said and I could tell she was smiling that smile of hers that always reminded me of Greg.

"See you tonight."

"See you tonight!"

A few hours later the pilot announced that we were officially in United States airspace. Dorito was sitting next to the window and I leaned over him to see the ground below, then I looked back at Laci and smiled. She was singing quietly to Lily in the seat behind me.

Very quietly. The important thing was that Lily could see Laci's lips moving as she sang. The song she was singing now was *Pon, Pon,* a Spanish song:

> *Pon, pon, pon,*
> *el dedito en el pilón.*

This translated into: *Put, put, put . . . your little finger in the cup.*

That's it. The whole song. Perhaps not the most exciting lyrics in the world, but it was my favorite because of the hand signal that went with it (not the sign language signals we were studying – just the regular ones that all Spanish kids learned with that song). When you sang "Pon, pon, pon," you were supposed to tap the index finger of one hand into the cupped palm of the other.

And that reminded me of Greg.

Ever since I'd known him he'd made up hand signals to remind his friends of things. Things that were funny or things that were important or things that he wanted us to think about. One day Laci had helped him make up one that the three of us could share. The index finger represented a nail and he would twist it into the palm of his other hand. It reminded us that Christ had loved us so much that He'd died for us. It also reminded us that we loved each other that much too.

So, *Pon, Pon* may not have been real riveting, but the hand signal that went with it reminded me of Greg, so I liked it a lot.

"We're finally in the United States," I told Dorito.

"I'm going to see my cousins!" he cried, clapping his hands. Dorito had been officially "ours" for only about six months and we hadn't been home in almost a year. My parents and Laci's parents had visited us in Mexico and met Dorito and Lily, but my sister and her family hadn't. Jessica and her husband, Christopher, had two children: Cassidy was about three years older than Dorito, and my nephew CJ was just a little bit younger than him. They'd video chatted and stuff, but they'd never actually met. Dorito could hardly wait.

"Relax," I said. "It's going to be a little while."

It would still be several hours before we'd land in Cavendish.

Cavendish.

Home.

I leaned my head back against the headrest. I wondered again, just briefly, why God was sending us home.

Maybe something terrible was going to happen to somebody that we loved and we were really going to need to be there. Or maybe something terrible was going to happen to one of us and we were going to need the support of all of our family and friends.

The scenario I was actually hoping for was that maybe God just felt sorry for us because of everything we'd already been through and He'd decided to give us a break. I closed my eyes and decided not to worry about it right now. We were over American soil and we were almost home. Everybody was happy and healthy and things were exactly the way I wanted them to be.

I was going to enjoy it while I could.

~ ~ ~

CHARLOTTE FLEW INTO my arms when we got to the terminal. After that, while her mom and my parents and Laci's parents greeted us, she was very careful to make a big deal out of meeting Dorito before Lily even though I could tell she was dying to hold Lily. First she knelt down next to Dorito and smiled at him.

"Hi," she said. "I'm Charlotte."

"I know," he said, sticking out his hand like a little man. "My daddy showed me pictures of you. I'm Dorito."

"I know you are," she said, shaking his hand.

"How do you know who I am?" he asked, astonished.

"Because he showed me pictures of you, too."

"He did?"

"Uh-huh."

"When?"

"On the computer," she replied.

"Ohhhh," he nodded as if it suddenly all made sense.

"Can I have a hug?" she asked him.

He smiled at her and nodded.

"I'm so glad you're here," she said as she hugged him and he smiled even more.

She stood up and hugged Laci who was holding Lily.

"Can I hold her?" Charlotte asked, already reaching her arms out to Lily.

"Sure you can," Laci said, handing her over.

Charlotte wrapped her arms around Lily and pressed her lips to the top of her head. She looked at her face and stroked her cheek and then held her tight.

"Oh! I love her!" Charlotte said breathlessly, kissing the top of her head again. She looked at us and smiled. "I love her! I love her! I love her!"

"What about me?" Dorito asked, tugging on her shirt.

Still holding Lily, Charlotte dropped to her knees again and wrapped one arm around Dorito.

"I love you, too," she said.

~ ~ ~

IT WAS THE end of July when we got back. My sister lived a few miles from our old neighborhood and let us stay in her basement . . . *again.*

"It's just until we can buy a place," I assured her. "Really. We won't be here long."

"Uh-huh," she said doubtfully, but I think she was just kidding. I was pretty sure that she loved having us stay with her.

When people started talking about throwing us a "Welcome Home" party, Laci and I decided instead to have a Second Annual Lasagna Bake-Off. Laci and I always loved a good bet and the previous August we'd had a contest to see who could make the best lasagna. I knew it wasn't going to be much of a contest this year either, but it was a good excuse to get everyone together again.

"Natalie's coming," Laci smiled two days beforehand. Natalie had finished seminary and was the youth pastor at a church in Denver.

"Tanner is too," I said. "He's bringing someone with him."

"Oh," she said, the smile slipping off of her face. "Are they serious?"

"I have no idea. He just asked if he could bring someone and I said yes."

"You should have told him no," she said. "There's no reason for him to 'bring someone' when Natalie's going to be here."

I rolled my eyes at her. She'd been trying to fix Tanner and Natalie up for years.

"I can call him back," I offered and this time she rolled her eyes at me.

The "someone" that Tanner brought was named Megan. I had a feeling they were pretty serious just because of how comfortable they acted around each other. Even though I knew it just about killed her, Laci dragged Megan off to introduce her to everybody (including Natalie). Tanner of course never moved far from the food table. He'd been a football player all through high school and college and it showed. He wasn't fat, he was just . . . *BIG*. He was about six foot seven and built like a brick wall.

"Your lasagna's disgusting," he said.

"Yeah. I know."

"Why don't you use a recipe or something?"

"I *did* use a recipe," I said.

"Maybe you should use a *different* recipe."

"So, you don't think I'm going to win this year either?" I asked, looking at the table. Laci's lasagna was *gone* . . . mine had been picked at.

"Are you serious?" he asked. "Laci's lasagna's great."

"I know," I sighed.

"So how long are you going to sponge off of Jessica?"

"Not too long," I said. "Why do you care?"

"Remember the Parkers?"

"Across the street from your old house?"

"Uh-huh."

"What about 'em?"

"Mr. Parker died last year . . ."

"Oh," I said. "I'm sorry to hear that."

The Parker's had always been really nice . . . letting us sled on the great hill in their front yard (even though their kids were grown) and giving us full-sized candy bars at Halloween instead of the miniature ones they gave everyone else (just because they knew us).

"My mom says Mrs. Parker's getting ready to put her house on the market . . ." (I *wasn't* sorry to hear that . . .), "and I don't know if you're looking for new construction or what, but . . ."

"No," I said. "I'd *love* to live in our old neighborhood."

"That's what I figured. I also figured Jordan could wander across the street every now and then and get you to help him with his math." Jordan was Tanner's youngest brother.

"Well, you know I'll help him with his math no matter where we live. How'd he do last year, anyway?"

We'd been home for the second half of Jordan's freshman year and I'd been able to tutor him a lot, but we'd been in Mexico for all of his sophomore year.

"He passed, but he did so bad on the state exam that they made him go to summer school."

"How's Chase doing?" I asked. Chase was their middle brother.

"Pretty good," Tanner said, nodding and chewing.

Just then Greg's mom came by holding Lily. She handed her to me and gave Tanner a hug.

"Ready to go back to school?" she asked him. Tanner was a coach at our old high school and classes would be starting in about a month.

"Did I ever leave?" he asked her. He was busy most of the summer with football training.

Lily was clutching at a hairclip and trying to gnaw on it. I took it from her, wiped it off on my jeans and then put it back in her hair. We didn't know how old she was for sure because she'd been abandoned (probably because her parents had figured out she was deaf), but we were thinking she was right about at a year.

"You wanna show Tanner and Mrs. White what you can do?" I asked her. Greg's mom was *always* going to be Mrs. White to me, no matter how many times she told me to call her Dana. I looked up at both of them.

"Watch," I said. I started singing to Lily and she watched my lips.

Pon, pon, pon,
el dedito en el pilón.

When I started singing it through the second time she pushed her index finger into her palm when I sang '*Pon, pon, pon*'.

"Did you see what she did?" I asked them. "That's the hand signal you're supposed to do when you sing that so it means she's reading my lips. She knows what I'm singing to her."

"That's wonderful!" Mrs. White exclaimed.

"Does she know any other signs?" Tanner wanted to know.

"It's not really a sign," I explained. "It's just something you do when you sing *Pon, Pon*. It's kind of like the Spanish version of patty-cake or something, but we *are* learning sign language."

"So are you going to talk to her in Spanish or English?" he asked.

"Both," I said. "We want her and Dorito to be bilingual."

"But if she learns to read lips," Tanner said, "won't that technically make her tri-lingual?"

"And if she learns sign language too," Mrs. White said, "then really she's going to be quadra-lingual . . ."

"I guess," I smiled. "I never really thought about it that way."

"I wonder if they'll make her take a foreign language in high school," Tanner mused. "I guess she could take German or something and then she'd be . . ."

"Quint-lingual?" I suggested.

Mrs. White laughed. "I don't think that's a word."

"Pent-lingual?"

Charlotte walked over to us.

"Can I hold her?" she asked me, reaching her hands out toward Lily.

12

"Yeah," I said, handing her over. "But don't let her eat her hair clip."

"You ready for school, Charlotte?" Tanner asked. Like his brother Jordan, Charlotte would be a junior at the high school.

"Do I have a choice?" she asked.

"Not unless I do."

"I don't know what you two are complaining about," I said. "Every year you get the *whole summer* off!"

"Oh, please," Tanner said. "This coming from a man who sits around the house all day, every day."

I was a structural engineer and I worked from home. I decided not to even dignify that with a response.

"What math are you taking?" I asked Charlotte.

"Pre-calc."

"Are you taking physics?"

"Of course I am," she said and I nodded my approval.

Lily started reaching toward Laci who was on the other side of the room.

"She wants her mommy," I told Charlotte.

"You want your mommy?" Charlotte asked her.

"You've gotta get her attention first," I told her because Lily had been looking away when Charlotte had spoken.

"Hey," Charlotte said, stroking Lily's cheek. Lily looked at her. "You wanna go see your mommy?"

Lily smiled at her and Charlotte headed toward Laci. Mrs. White started to follow, but stopped and turned back to me.

"Oh, David?"

"Yeah?"

"What did you *do* to that lasagna?" she asked, pointing to the table.

"Oh, go away," I said and she grinned at me before she left.

I loved being home.

That night in bed I told Laci what Tanner had said about the Parker's house.

"We could go by and talk to her if you want," I said.

"Yeah," she said. "Let's check it out." We'd hardly seen any For Sale signs in our old neighborhood since we'd been home.

"I was talking to Ashlyn tonight," she said after a minute. "Guess what?"

Ashlyn, Natalie and Laci had all been best friends in high school. Ashlyn was married, lived a few miles away, and was the youth director at our church.

"She's pregnant."

Ashlyn already had a little girl named Amelia who was a little bit younger than Dorito.

"No."

"What then?"

"Well, she said that they had a big summer festival and invited all the youth groups from the other churches to come and none of the kids from Tanner's church came."

"How come?"

"Apparently they really don't even *have* a youth group. Ashlyn thinks that they don't have anyone willing to lead it."

"Oh."

We lay there quietly for a few moments.

Sometimes I'm so dense. You'd think after being married to Laci for four years and knowing her for my *whole* life that I'd have seen what was coming next.

"You know what I was thinking?" she finally said.

"What?"

"Maybe we could help out . . ."

"Whatdaya mean?"

"I mean like maybe we could help lead their youth group."

14

"*What?*"

"You know . . . they need someone and there's really no reason we couldn't do it . . ."

"Except that we don't go to that church!"

"We could change . . ."

"What? No way Laci! We've been going to our church all our lives and we just got back here! I don't want to leave!"

"Well they need someone, Dave . . ."

"Well, then let someone from their church lead it."

"But no one will. These kids really need someone. Think how important youth group was to us. What if Greg's dad hadn't of come along and started up a youth group for us?"

I sighed. I was going to keep arguing for a while, but I already knew how this was going to turn out.

"Look, Laci," I said. "I've got enough to do without the responsibility of leading a youth group."

"But we'll do it together!" she insisted. "It won't be hard if we're both doing it."

"Right," I said. "And who's going to watch Dorito and Lily while were doing youth group stuff? You know as well as I do that I'm the one who's going to wind up taking them everywhere and doing everything with them because you're going to be home with Dorito and Lily."

"No!" she said. "My parents can watch 'em and your parents and Jessica and we can hire a sitter . . . *really!* You won't wind up doing it alone."

"Uh-huh."

The *first* thing I wound up doing alone was taking six kids from Tanner's church to Six Flags three weeks later. Mr. White had taken us on the same trip when he'd formed our youth group, so I figured it was the thing to do.

"Can I turn on the radio?" Stephanie asked me. She was a tenth grader and was sitting next to me in the front passenger seat. The five other kids who'd signed up to go were all sitting behind us in Laci's van, including Tanner's brother, Jordan.

"Sure!" I said. When Mr. White had taken us I'd been twelve years old. We'd listened to contemporary Christian music the whole way and I hadn't known a single song. I wasn't going to feel left out this time though; it was all I listened to now.

The song that was playing when Stephanie turned on the radio was Casting Crown's *Every Man*. It was an old song, but still came on the radio every now and then. It had always been one of my favorites and I was happy to hear it. Then I was dismayed when she hit the scan button.

"AC/DC!" someone shouted from the back seat. "Stop it there!" Stephanie punched another button and before I knew it everyone was singing *Highway to Hell*.

Everyone, that is, except for Jordan.

When I glanced back at him in the mirror he was stuffing earphones from his MP3 player into his ears. He leaned his head back and closed his eyes and I spent yet another drive to Six Flags not knowing the words to any of the songs.

When we got to Six Flags I made all the kids line up and call my number so they'd have it on their phones and I'd have theirs too. Then I told them we'd meet back at the entrance at five and I let them go off on their own.

After wandering around for about two hours I called Laci.

"How're you doing?" she asked.

"Miserable."

16

"Why?"

"Well," I said, "did you know that 3-D shows can cause motion sickness?"

"Of course they can. They've got little warning signs out front."

"Yeah," I said. "'*Little*' is the key word there."

"How sick did you get?" she laughed.

"Not too bad. After I figured out what was going on I closed my eyes. 'Course the seats were moving all around too and that didn't help any. I should have known something was up when I had to put on a seatbelt."

She laughed again.

"I'm sorry," she said, not sounding sorry at all.

"You owe me, big time, Laci," I said and she laughed one more time.

After an hour or so I was feeling normal. I walked around and as I passed a restaurant, I realized it was the same one that Greg and I had gone to when his dad had brought *our* youth group to Six Flags fourteen years ago. That day had really been the start of my friendship with Greg. Suddenly I decided I was hungry.

I was staring off at nothing, eating my cheeseburger and fries, when I realized that Jordan was standing in front of me, waving his hand in front of my face.

"Earth to Dave," he said.

"Oh," I said, blinking at him. "Hi."

"Where were *you* just then?" he asked.

"Childhood . . ."

"Oh," he said. "Sorry to interrupt. Mind if I sit down?"

He was balancing a tray of food in one hand and trying to keep a giant stuffed panda off the floor with the other.

"No," I said. "Help yourself."

I pulled out the chair next to me so he could set the panda down. It barely fit.

"What's up with, uh . . ." I pointed to the bear.

"Cuddles?"

"You named it 'Cuddles'?"

"No," he said. "That's what the tag says."

"Okay," I said. "So what's up with Cuddles?"

"I won him."

"You must be very happy."

"I'm going to give it to Dorito," he explained.

"You *really* don't have to do that . . ."

"No problem," he grinned.

"Gee," I said, rolling my eyes. "Thanks."

"You're welcome," he nodded, holding up his drink as if in a toast.

"So *why* did you win Cuddles?"

"Pitching," he said. "Every time you throw one over seventy-five miles per hour you win and then you keep trading up."

"So how much did ol' Cuddles here wind up costing you?"

He thought for a moment.

"About twenty-five bucks."

"You probably could have *bought* him for that," I said.

"I didn't do it because I wanted a bear," he said in a tone that clearly implied I was an idiot. "I just wanted to see how fast I could throw."

"Uh-huh, sure ya did," I said, nodding my head at him.

"So have you been having fun so far?" he asked, taking a huge bite of pizza.

"Thrill a minute," I said. "Where's everybody else?"

"I don't know," he shrugged. "I was with the guys for a while but they got sick of watching me pitch so they took off."

"What about the girls?"

"I haven't seen 'em since we got here."

"Oh, well," I said. "I'm sure they're having a good time."

18

Jordan nodded as he started on his second slice of pizza. I wondered briefly if he was going to wind up as big as Tanner. He was already taller than I was, but that probably wasn't saying much.

"So," he said after a while. "Tanner says you won't mind helping me in math again this year?"

"No," I said. "That'd be great."

"I've gotta do really good this year. The scouts aren't even going to look at me in the spring if my grades aren't good enough for me to get into college."

"Are you taking geometry?"

"In the spring," he nodded.

"Good," I said. "I *love* geometry!"

"And I'm taking a math SAT prep class this fall."

"That'll be fun too," I said. "No problem."

He shook his head at me. "You're so weird."

"Yeah, I know," I said, pushing my tray away from me and wiping my mouth. "That's what Laci keeps telling me."

"Are you going to eat the rest of your fries?" he asked.

"You can have 'em."

"Are you sure?"

"Knock yourself out," I said. It was *just* like eating with Tanner.

I worked on my milkshake while he finished off his pizza and my fries. Then he went back to the counter and got a milkshake because mine looked so good.

"What are you going to do now?" he asked when he got back to the table.

"Wander around for four hours I guess," I said, looking at my watch.

"Do you think you could take him out to the van?" he asked, pointing at Cuddles. "Ya know . . . so I don't have to carry him around all day?"

"Sure," I said. "Where are you going next?"

"I'm gonna go win something for Lily," he grinned.

"Oh, brother."

I went along and watched Jordan pitch for a while. He was pretty good . . . a lot better than he'd been when I'd seen him play as a freshman. I figured the scouts were definitely going to be interested in him. His arm was getting tired though and it cost him over thirty bucks to win a giant stuffed dog for Lily. After he was done I lugged them both back to the van and by the time I waved my stamped hand under a black light to re-enter the park I only had two and a half more hours to kill.

~ ~ ~

SHORTLY AFTER OUR lasagna bake-off, Laci and I had gone by and talked to Mrs. Parker. Not only did she remember us, but she seemed thrilled that we were interested in buying her house because she "really didn't want a bunch of strangers traipsing through it". The wall-to-wall carpet was outdated and worn in spots, but we didn't care. The builder was friends with my dad and we knew there were hardwoods underneath.

When Dorito started kindergarten in the fall, we were still living with Jessica, but by the middle of September we were able to move in. On our first Saturday in our new house Laci called to me from the living room.

"What's wrong?" I hollered back.

"Dorito's gone!"

"He's fine," I assured Laci, walking down the hall toward her.

Laci said he wasn't in the house or the yard, but for some reason I wasn't worried. Laci wasn't so calm and she went out into the back yard and started calling for him while I went into the front.

Across the street I saw Jordan step into his side yard and wave at me.

"He's over here!"

"He's across the street," I yelled to Laci over the house and she came around our side yard with Lily on her hip. Together, we walked over to Jordan's house.

Jordan and his mom were the only ones living in the house that Tanner had grown up in. Their middle brother Chase had moved to Chicago shortly after he'd graduated from high school and Tanner was living on the other side of town. Their dad had walked out on them about six years ago.

I'd spent hundreds of hours in their backyard when I was growing up, but it looked a lot different now. The shop door was wide open and I noticed that all of their dad's woodworking stuff was gone and the shop had been turned into a mini-gym. There was a weight bench, a treadmill, a stationary bike and a stair-stepper. On the side of the shop there was a large cement pad with a basketball goal and on the edge of the yard was a full-sized soccer goal. A tire, suspended from a tree with a tarp hanging behind it, hung over the ground that was littered with baseballs. There was even a mini driving range with a net to catch golf balls.

"Good grief," I said. Jordan just grinned at me.

"You are not to *ever* leave our house again without asking Mommy or Daddy first," Laci was saying, shaking her finger in Dorito's face. "Do you understand me?"

He nodded at her solemnly.

Jordan turned serious.

"I'm sorry," he said. "I figured you guys had told him he could come over here."

"Don't worry about it," I said, looking around. "Boy, Jordan . . . I'm disappointed in you. Where's your batting cage?"

"Trust me," he said, smiling again. "If I could figure out how to pay for a pitching machine I'd have one."

"What's a batting cage?" Dorito wanted to know. Jordan told him what it was and explained to him why he'd need a pitching machine to use it.

"If you build one," Dorito said, "my daddy'll come over here and throw balls for you."

"Yeah, right," I laughed. "I'm going to get myself trapped in a cage with Jordan smacking balls at my head at 200 miles an hour."

"Come on," Laci said. "We'd better go."

"I don't wanna go!" Dorito cried. "I don't wanna go!"

"I'm sure Jordan doesn't need you over here pestering him . . ." I began.

"Actually he's fine if you wanna leave him here," Jordan said, pointing toward the tire. "He was running balls back to me. He's kind of helpful."

Dorito beamed.

"Are you sure?" Laci asked.

"Sure, I'm sure," Jordan nodded. "I'll bring him home when we're done."

Laci and I took Lily back across the street, listening to the *thwack* of baseballs hitting the backdrop. I glanced over at Laci; she was laughing.

"What?"

"I was just thinking," she said, shaking her head, "that when the testosterone was being handed out, that family got a double dose."

~ ~ ~

WE WOUND UP seeing a lot of Jordan. He'd already started getting help from me in math once or twice a week while we were still living at Jessica's, but after we moved in across the street from him he began coming over even more. I also started giving Jordan a lift to youth group every week because between him and his mom, they only had one car. The first evening we rode together I had the radio on and Jordan started singing along.

"You listen to this station?" I asked him.

"Yeah," he said. "Why do you act so surprised?"

"Well, because when we went to Six Flags nobody wanted to listen to Christian music."

"I did," he said. "I listen to it all the time."

"Really? How come you didn't say anything?"

"I don't know," he shrugged.

"You should've said something," I told him. "The other kids might have gotten into it."

"Oh, it's okay."

"No . . . I mean you could've been an example, you know? That's how I started listening to it – because my friends were listening to it all the time. You should have said something."

"*You* didn't say anything," he said, looking at me. "You just let 'em change the station."

"Touché."

"I usually just keep my mouth shut," he went on.

"I noticed."

"We'll gang up on 'em next time," he said.

"Sure we will."

Before long, whenever we heard the sounds of barbells clanging or basketballs pounding on the pavement, Dorito would beg to go over and see Jordan. Laci and I kept trying to discourage him, figuring that Jordan would rather not spend his free time with a five-year-old, but Jordan insisted he didn't mind. I think he was just trying to be nice since I was helping him so much with his math and I wouldn't let him pay me.

"That's not right, is it?" Jordan asked one evening, showing me a problem he had just finished.

"No."

"I hate math!" he said, laying his head down on the desk. "I hate it, I hate it, I *hate* it!"

"You know what your problem is, Jordan?"

He rolled his head to look up at me.

"What?"

"Your problem is that you beat yourself up every time you make one little mistake. I mean you set this up perfect – you did everything right until you got to right here," I said, tapping his paper. "Look at everything that you did right! Last week you didn't even know where to start on this kind of problem."

"But it's still *wrong*."

"Okay," I said. "So you made a mistake. Everybody makes mistakes."

"You don't . . ."

"Right. Look," I said, pointing to my trashcan on the other side of the room. "Watch this . . ."

I crumpled up his paper into a tight ball and tossed it. It sailed toward the wall, swished through the miniature basketball net that I had mounted on my wall, and landed in the trashcan.

I crumpled up another piece of paper and handed it to him.

"You try."

He tossed it toward the net but missed. The paper landed on the floor.

"See, I hardly ever miss," I smiled. "You know why?"

He shook his head.

"Because every time I make a mistake I just throw it away," I said. "I've had lots and lots of practice."

By the middle of October, Jordan was coming over almost every weeknight to work on his math. By now he really didn't need tons of help. He worked quietly most of the time and I actually got a lot of work done too. I think he just liked having me around in case he got stuck on a problem.

"You've got tomorrow off," Jordan informed me one Wednesday evening.

"Why?"

"Tanner and I are in a racquetball tournament."

"Racquetball?"

"Yeah," he nodded. "You ever play?"

"I tried it one time . . ."

"You didn't like it?"

"Your brother tried to teach me," I said, tilting my head at him.

"Oh," he nodded.

Enough said.

Just then my phone rang. It was Charlotte.

"Here," I said to Jordan, pointing to a problem before I opened my phone. "Start graphing this real quick . . ."

He set to work.

"What's up, Charlotte?" I asked.

"Can you help me with a math problem?"

"That seems to be my specialty."

"Huh?"

"Never mind." I wasn't sure if Jordan would appreciate Charlotte knowing that he was getting help in a class she'd taken the honors version of and made an "A" in two years ago. "What's the problem?"

She read it out loud to me and I wrote it down.

"Have you tried my mom?" I asked her. My mom taught math at the high school.

"She's at choir practice."

"Oh, yeah."

"What's the matter?" she teased. "Can't you figure it out?"

"I can figure it out just fine," I said defensively. "It might take me awhile though . . . I haven't done this in six years. Have you got the answer?"

"All real numbers greater than zero, x is not zero."

"Alright. I'll call you back in a little bit."

"Thanks."

I hung up and frowned at the paper. Jordan looked at the problem too.

"What is *that?*" he asked, furrowing his brow.

"Pre-calc." It probably looked like gibberish to him. It almost looked like gibberish to me.

"Can you do that?"

"I'm going to solve this if it kills me," I told him and he smiled. He worked quietly while I rifled through books on my shelf and flipped pages.

"This is one of those stupid things you never use again after you learn it," I muttered after about ten minutes.

"Kind of like geometry?" he asked and I smirked at him.

After about a half of an hour I apologized to Jordan for taking so long.

"No problem," he said. "It's kind of nice to have somebody else being lost besides me."

"I'm not lost!" I cried. "I just don't see how they're getting all real numbers greater than zero . . . I keep getting positive one."

"Sounds like you're lost to me."

I glared at him.

Ten minutes later Charlotte called again. I dreaded answering the phone.

"I haven't had a chance to work on it yet," I lied, winking at Jordan. He laughed.

"Well, don't bother," she said. "Your mom called me back . . . I got it."

"*You got it?*" I was going to have to call my mom as soon as I hung up.

"Yeah," she said. "They printed the wrong answer in the back of the book."

"It's not all real numbers greater than zero?"

"No, it's positive one."

"That's what I kept getting!!"

"I thought you hadn't worked on it yet . . ."

"*Goodnight*, Charlotte."

~ ~ ~

ONE DAY JORDAN was standing in our kitchen, eating a brownie, while he and Laci complained about all the rules in math.

"That's the *beauty* of math!" I argued. "It's either right or it's wrong! All you've gotta do is follow the rules and you can't miss!"

They glanced at each other and I could tell I was never going to convince either one of them.

"Is it okay if I read a story to Lily before we start?" Jordan asked.

"Sure," Laci said. "Her books are in her room."

"I brought one," he answered, reaching into his backpack and pulling out a children's book.

"I wanna read it too," Dorito begged.

"Okay," Jordan said, walking into the living room. He sat on the floor with his back against the couch. Dorito sat down facing him and Laci put Lily on Dorito's lap so that she could see Jordan's lips. Jordan opened the book so it was right side up for them.

Then he started reading it.

And *signing* it.

Laci and I looked at each other quizzically and then sat down on the floor to listen and watch too.

I couldn't believe it. It wasn't a particularly long story, but it must have taken him a while to learn all the signs and he did about four or five that I didn't even know yet. Lily looked up and down from Jordan to the book and I think she really liked having somebody besides me or Laci reading and signing to her for a change.

"That was fantastic," Laci told him when he'd finished.

"Did I make any mistakes?" he asked, looking up at us.

She shook her head at him and he smiled.

"How'd you learn that?" I asked. "The Internet?" You could go online and learn a lot of sign language, but it wasn't the same as having someone teach you. Laci and I went to classes once a week at the community college *and* we hired someone to come in and work with all of us twice a week.

"No," he said, shaking his head and looking down at Lily who was reaching for the book. "One of the E.C. teachers at school knows it and I had her show me."

"I can't believe you did that, Jordan," Laci said.

"Well," he shrugged, letting Lily have the book, "I think her neighbors should know how to communicate with her."

"That was really nice of you," I told him.

"It's the least I can do after all the help you've been giving me," he said. "Speaking of which, I got totally lost in class today."

"Well then," I said, standing up, "let's get to it."

"Okay," he sighed, looking at Laci as he stood up too. "By the way, sign language is *way* easier to learn than math."

"Tell me about it," Laci laughed.

~ ~ ~

ONE MORNING AT the end of October, Laci had taken Lily over to her mother's house so she could run some errands without her. I was hard at work, taking advantage of the quiet, when I heard Laci come in the front door. I heard her because she *slammed* the door as hard as she could . . . so hard that my hand jumped and my template moved and my pencil gouged a hole in the graph paper I was working on. It was a wonder I ever got any work done.

I was going to crumple it up dramatically in front of her, but she stormed into my office with such vehemence that I thought better of it.

"What's up?"

"He is *LIVING* with her!" she yelled at me.

"Who's living with who?"

"Tanner is *LIVING* with Megan. They aren't just *dating* . . . they're *living* together!"

I had absolutely no idea what to say. The only thing that was coming to my mind was '*So?*' and I had a feeling that wasn't going to go over too well right now.

She glared at me.

"Did you know about this?"

I shook my head at her.

"I cannot believe this," she said, shaking her head in disgust.

I just sat there quietly looking at her because I was pretty sure that anything I said was going to be wrong.

"Well?" she asked.

"Well, what?"

"Aren't you going to say something?"

"I . . . I really don't know what to say."

"I am so mad at him," she said.

"Why?" I finally asked.

31

"Why?" she yelled. "*Why* am I mad at him? I can't believe you don't know why I'm mad at him!"

I knew it! I *knew* no matter what I said it was going to be wrong.

"Are you jealous?" I asked. Tanner and Laci had gone to the prom together when they were juniors and I was hoping a little bit of humor might lighten things up a bit.

It didn't.

"He is *living* with her, David!" she yelled again. "I cannot believe this. What's wrong with him? He knows better!"

"He knows better?"

"Yes! He knows better. They shouldn't be living together."

"Laci," I said, well aware I was probably getting ready to make a mistake. "He's twenty-six years old."

"So?"

"So he's old enough to make his own decisions."

"And this is what he decides to do? It's wrong, David! They shouldn't be living together."

I waved my hand dismissively at her. "They probably just aren't ready to get married yet . . . I don't think it's that big of a deal."

"NOT A BIG DEAL?"

Okay, obviously it *was* a big deal.

"If they aren't ready to get married," she went on, "then they shouldn't be *living* together. I am so mad at him right now, I just can't believe it."

I couldn't believe how mad she was either.

"Listen, Laci," I said. "I just think maybe you're blowing this out of proportion a little bit. Lots of people live together before they get married."

"Mike and Danica are waiting until they get married . . ."

"Well, maybe they aren't living together," I said, "but–"

"They aren't doing *anything* together!"

"Oh, come *on*, Laci. How could you possibly know that?" We'd met Danica once and we hadn't even seen her and Mike since we'd been back from Mexico.

"Because of her ring."

"What? Her engagement ring?"

"No . . . on her other hand. She was wearing a True Love Waits ring."

I must have had a blank look on my face because she went on.

"It's a program that encourages people to make a commitment to wait until they're married."

No wonder Laci had liked Danica so much.

"I don't remember seeing one of those rings on *Mike*," I said.

"I *guarantee* you they're waiting."

I looked at her skeptically.

"Call Mike!" she dared, pointing at my phone. "Call him and see!"

"No," I said. "That's okay. I believe you."

Not really.

"Look, Laci," I went on. "I don't wanna get yelled at or anything, but I just don't understand why you're so upset."

"He's a teacher!" I was getting yelled at anyway. "He's supposed to be setting an example for his students! They should *not* be living with each other!"

"What's going on, Laci? Since when are you so judgmental?"

My words stopped her and then her eyes filled up with tears.

"This is Tanner we're talking about," she finally said, softly. "He's our friend . . . I'm worried about him."

"I don't think you need to worry about him just because he's living with Megan."

"He's in trouble, David."

"You're making too much out of this," I said, reaching for her and pulling her toward me. "You need to relax."

"You mark my words, David," she said, shaking her head before she put it on my shoulder. "Tanner's in trouble."

The next few days were full of nothing except for Laci *not* relaxing.

She recounted how she'd run into Megan at the bank and how they'd gotten to talking and how she just couldn't *believe* it when she realized they were living together . . . how she'd tried to hold it together and not let on to Megan how *shocked* and *upset* she was.

She ranted and raved, informing me about how much more likely people were to get divorced if they lived together first. *Don't they know that?*

Tanner was headed down the wrong road fast . . . she was sure of it. *We need to be praying for him.*

And she bugged me relentlessly, asking me what I knew about Tanner's relationship with Christ. *Do you have any idea how he could have possibly gotten so far away from God?*

I have to confess that I actually knew almost nothing about Tanner's relationship with Christ. This was especially bad since I'd known him *forever* – literally for all of our lives. We'd been in school together from preschool through high school, in Scouts, and in every sport we'd ever belonged to except for when he and Mike had abandoned soccer in favor of football and I'd started swimming while they'd played basketball. Sure, when Greg had moved to town just before the seventh grade we'd paired off a little . . . Tanner and Mike wound up spending more time with each other just like Greg and I did. But still, he'd always been one of my *best* friends. How could I not know what to say when Laci asked me about his relationship with Christ?

Tanner's family had belonged to a different church than the one that Laci and Mike and Greg and I had all gone to together. That accounted for part of the reason that I knew more about their relationships with God than I did Tanner's.

But only part.

Looking back now, trying to come up with an answer to Laci's questions, I realized that Tanner and I had really never talked about it.

And as I silently admitted this to myself, I started feeling awfully ashamed.

The next Saturday morning I was on the couch watching TV with Dorito. We were flipping channels, landed on a hunting show, and the next thing I knew we were in front of the computer ordering a camouflage jacket, pants and boots for Dorito.

"Why?" Laci asked when she found out what we'd done.

"I'm taking him hunting," I said.

"I don't think that's a good idea."

"It's not like I'm going to let him carry a gun or anything," I assured her.

"I don't think it's a good idea," she said again.

Now before you go getting the idea that Laci was all anti-gun or didn't want us killing Bambi or something like that, let me assure you that's not the case. Her dad was a big hunter and Laci had gone with him a lot when he duck hunted on the Mississippi. In fact, she'd been younger than Dorito the first time she went.

And one time – in high school – Tanner's dad had taken us dove hunting and she'd come along. It had been Tanner's dad, Tanner and his brothers (Chase and Jordan), Greg, Mike, me and Laci. We'd teased her the whole drive up there, but then she and Tanner's dad had been the only ones to get their limits. I think I'd only gotten five and I'd used about two boxes of shells to do it.

No, Laci wasn't against hunting at all. The reason she didn't want me to take Dorito is because she knew that I wasn't going to take him alone.

She knew I'd be going with Tanner.

Tanner had all the good *stuff* you needed to go hunting – a truck, a hunting dog and (most importantly) the permission of local landowners. All I had was a 16 gauge and a four-door sedan. Somehow I didn't think I was going to get too far all by myself.

I met Tanner at his house because I really didn't want Laci near him when there was a gun around.

"Hola!" Tanner said when he opened the door.

"Hola," Dorito yawned, (it was five in the morning). I let him slump on Tanner's couch while I moved his booster seat into Tanner's truck. When I got back inside, Tanner's Springer spaniel was licking Dorito's face.

"This is T.D.," Tanner told Dorito.

"Hola, T.D.," Dorito mumbled, burying his face into the couch.

"Touch Down?" I guessed.

"Tanner's Dog," he grinned.

I threw my gun and cooler into the bed of his truck and T.D. jumped into the back seat. I retrieved Dorito off the couch, did up his seatbelt and then we took off.

We talked for a little while about where we were going and the farmer who owned the land we'd be hunting on and how his grandson had been on the high school's football team last spring.

"How's Megan?" I finally asked, trying to sound casual.

36

"Fine," he said, pausing before going on. "She told me she ran into Laci a couple of weeks ago."

"Yeah," I said. "Laci mentioned that too."

"I'll bet she did," he said, glancing at me.

We rode in silence for a few moments.

"You could've given me the heads up," I told him.

"Probably should have," he admitted.

"So are you two gonna get married?"

"I doubt it."

"Why not?"

"I don't wanna marry her."

I wanted to ask him why in the world he was *living* with her if he didn't want to marry her, but instead I just said again, "Why not?"

"She wants to have kids . . . I don't."

"Why don't you want to have kids? It's *great* having kids."

"I know what kids are like," he said. "I work with kids all day long."

"It's different when they're yours," I assured him, glancing back at Dorito. He was sound asleep in his booster seat with T.D.'s head on his lap.

"Uh-huh."

"I'm serious, Tanner. It's *completely* different."

He just shook his head.

"Everything's so screwed up," he said. "There's no *way* I'd bring a kid into this world the way everything is."

"Everything's screwed up? Whatdaya mean?"

He looked at me like I was insane.

"*What do I mean?* I mean global warming, pollution, terrorist attacks, drugs . . . you name it. Plus all our rights are getting taken away from us. We probably aren't going to get to go hunting much longer because guns are going to be illegal and then all we're going to have are a bunch of criminals who have guns and we won't have any way to defend ourselves. There's no *way* I'd bring a kid into this world."

"I had no idea you were so miserable."

"Yeah, well," he said. "You haven't been around much."

I stared at him and he glanced at me.

"Oh, get that look off your face," he said. "I'm only kidding. I just have no desire to sit around playing *Pon, Pon* all day, that's all."

"First of all," I said, "you don't play *Pon, Pon*, you *sing* it."

"Whatever . . ."

"I can't believe you don't want to have kids," I said, shaking my head. "You don't know what you're missing."

"Uh-huh."

"You know what Greg would do if he were here?" I asked.

"I can't even begin to imagine . . ."

"He'd give you the *Pon, Pon* signal every chance he got," I said, pushing my finger into my palm, "to try to convince you how great it is to have kids."

"You're probably exactly right," Tanner agreed, laughing.

"I could do it instead," I offered. "I'm getting pretty good at hand signals you know."

"Don't bother," he said. "I really *don't* want to do the family thing."

We rode along quietly for a few minutes and I decided I was going to do it anyway.

"So what'd Laci say?" he finally asked, breaking the silence.

"About what?"

He looked at me and sighed.

I hesitated for a second because Laci was already mad at Tanner. I really didn't want him mad at her too.

"She's just worried about you, Tanner."

"Are *you*?"

"Should I be?"

"Nope."

38

"Well then let's just go kill some pheasants."

"Yeah," he said, smiling at me. "Like *you're* going to be able to hit a pheasant."

I actually did hit a pheasant . . . I know because I saw a few feathers fluttering down as it flew away, otherwise unharmed. Tanner got two.

"Does he always sleep this much?" Tanner asked, looking at Dorito in his mirror as we drove home.

"Just when he gets up at four-thirty in the morning and chases a dog around all day."

"I hope he had fun," Tanner said.

"Oh, he did . . . trust me. He had a great time."

"Good."

"Ya know," I said, "I've been thinking about something you said this morning."

"What's that?"

"About how you said the world's too screwed up for you to ever wanna have a kid."

His jaw clenched slightly and his fists seemed to tighten on the steering wheel.

"You're going to make a big deal out of this, aren't you?" he asked.

"A big deal out of what?"

"Everything."

"No, I'm not."

"I really don't need you preaching to me the way Mike does."

"Mike preaches to you?"

"You know what I mean."

"Ummm . . . no, really I don't," I said.

"Do you miss Mexico?"

"Wow, Tanner," I said. "That was really smooth. Way to change the subject."

"Do you miss it?" he persisted.

"No," I said, letting him win. "I don't miss it one bit. We've got Dorito and Lily and I don't care if we ever set foot in Mexico again."

"He's a good kid," Tanner said, looking in his mirror at Dorito again.

"Yeah," I agreed. "He's great."

"He made a nice retrieve on that one pheasant," Tanner laughed. "T.D. never even saw it go down, but Dorito ran right to it. If you could teach him how to flush birds you wouldn't even need a dog."

"Remember when your dad took us hunting and he had Jordan and Chase retrieving doves for us?"

"Yeah," Tanner laughed, "and one landed in the pond so they were both racing out there trying to swim with their boots on."

"Man, it was hot that day!" I said. "I remember I felt like jumping right in there with them."

"It was fun though."

"It was a lot of fun," I agreed. "I always had fun hunting and fishing with your dad."

"Yeah."

"You guys ever hear from him?"

"No," Tanner said and I saw his jaw clench and his fists tighten again so I decided to just change the subject myself this time.

"Chase still doing construction?"

"Yep."

"He like it?"

"I guess so."

"Does he ever talk about going to college?"

40

"He barely made it through high school," Tanner said, tilting his head at me. "Too bad you weren't around to help him like you're helping Jordan. I thought Jordan was headed the same way, but he's sailing right along now."

"I like working with him."

"Just 'cause it gives you an excuse to do more math," Tanner smiled.

"Possibly."

"You're such a nerd," he said, shaking his head. "Have you got a slide rule in your shooting vest or just a calculator?"

"Just a calculator. Two actually . . ."

"You're serious aren't you?"

"There's one on my phone and one on my GPS."

"You're such a nerd," he repeated.

"Better to be a rich nerd than a dumb jock," I murmured under my breath, just loud enough for him to hear me.

"What's that?" Tanner asked, cupping his hand to his ear.

"Nothing," I said, suppressing a smile.

It was the friendly banter that Tanner and I had engaged in all our lives. It was fun and it was meaningless and it was what we did for the rest of the ride home.

It was what Tanner wanted.

Dorito's nap while we drove was enough to energize him and he bounded into our house swinging the pheasants that Tanner had insisted we take (so that *he* wouldn't have to clean them).

"Look what we got!" Dorito shouted, holding them up to Laci.

"Oh, wow!" Laci said. "Did you kill those?"

"No. Uncle Tanner did."

"Uncle Tanner did, huh?"

"Yep. Daddy missed."

"Imagine that."

"I didn't exactly miss . . ."

"He got a feather," Dorito explained.

"Oh," Laci said. "Too bad we can't eat feathers. Why don't you go put those down by the sink in the basement and I'm sure Daddy'll come down there in a minute and give you a big biology lesson, okay?"

"Okay," he said, heading toward the stairs.

"Well?" she asked, turning to me when Dorito was gone.

"I didn't give it a far enough lead."

She sighed. "You know that's not what I mean. How'd it go?"

"It was great . . . we had a great time."

"How was Tanner?"

"He was fine."

"David . . ."

She looked at me with such concern that I finally quit playing around.

"I don't know what's going on with him, Laci," I admitted.

"What happened?"

"Nothing happened . . . he's just the same old Tanner."

"But I was right, wasn't I?"

"I don't know."

"What are you going to do?"

"I don't know," I said again, but that wasn't entirely true.

I knew I was going to talk to Mike.

~ ~ ~

THE NEXT DAY after church I called Mike.

"Hey, Dave."

"Hey, Mike."

"What's up?"

"Oh, nothing much. You wanna get together for lunch or something this week?"

He was in his last year of medical school, *four* hours away.

"Oh, boy," he sighed. "This sounds good."

"No, it's not that big of a deal," I assured him. "I'll come up there. I haven't been to Minnesota in a long time."

"When are you coming?"

"What's good for you?"

"I don't have anything after three on Thursday."

"Then I guess I'll see you Thursday," I said.

"I'll send you some directions," he said.

"Okay. See you then."

"Bye."

We decided to meet at the McDonald's near the university because it was easy to find. I made good time and got there early so I ordered a drink, sat down in a corner, and pulled out my computer. I was reading my messages when I heard a woman's voice.

"David?"

I looked up. It took me a second to recognize her, but it was Mike's fiancé, Danica.

"Oh! Hi!" I said, standing up to hug her.

"Mike's going to be late," she said as she sat down across from me.

"Oh, okay."

"He didn't want to just call you and have you sitting here alone for an hour," she said, glancing at my computer, "but it looks like you have plenty to keep you busy."

"I've always got plenty to keep me busy."

"You want to get back to work?"

"No," I said, closing it. "I can do this anytime."

Her phone went off and she reached into her briefcase. As she pulled it out and slid it open I noticed her rings . . . her engagement ring *and* her True Love Waits ring. Laci really burned me sometimes.

"Hey . . . yeah . . . okay . . . alright . . . sounds good . . . no problem . . . okay . . . love you too."

She put her phone away.

"He wants me to take you to his apartment."

"Is everything okay?"

"There was a house fire and he got called out." (Mike had been an E.M.T. ever since he'd been in undergraduate school.)

"Was anybody hurt?"

"I don't know," she said, shaking her head. "Every year when the weather turns cold people start setting their houses on fire, trying to stay warm."

"Maybe . . . maybe I should come back some other time."

"No," she said. "This is typical. He gets calls all the time."

I looked at her uncertainly.

"I promise. He's glad you came."

"Okay."

"Come on," she said. "You can follow me."

After we'd weaved through town and finally arrived at Mike's apartment Danica pulled her keys out and opened his door.

"Have a seat," she said. "You want something to drink?"

"No, I'm good."

Her phone went off again.

"He's got wireless here . . ." she offered before she answered.

"Okay."

I opened up my computer again while she talked to Mike.

"He wants to know if you want Chinese," she asked me.

"Sure."

"What do you want?"

"He knows what to get."

I went back to my computer and after she was done talking to Mike she went into the kitchen and washed dishes. I was closing the lid when she came into the living room, wiping her hands on a dish towel.

"Wouldn't you think that someone who's almost a doctor would know that it's unsanitary to leave dirty dishes lying around?" she asked.

"He was probably letting them soak."

"Right . . . I'm sure that'll be his excuse."

"He just needs a wife," I smiled.

"That's an understatement," she said, smiling back.

"Have you guys set a date?"

"Yeah . . . the weekend before Easter."

"Good. Am I invited?"

"Oh, you're invited. You might even be *in* it," she said, smiling again and giving me a wink, "but I'd better let Mike talk to you about that."

"Okay."

Almost on cue the door opened and Mike stepped in, smiling at both of us. Danica hugged him.

"I did your dishes," she said.

"There were dishes?"

"Yes . . . there were dishes."

"I told her you were probably letting them soak," I said.

"Yeah," he agreed. "I was letting them soak."

"Uh-huh."

Mike and I greeted each other and then Danica went into the bathroom. Mike started unpacking cartons of food and opened a package of paper plates. He only put two down on the table and when Danica came out of the bathroom she kissed him goodbye.

"Good to see you again, Dave," she said, putting on her coat.

"You can stay . . ." I said.

"No, I'm going to leave you two alone. I'll see you again soon."

"Bye."

After she closed the door I looked at Mike.

"This is *not* that big of a deal . . . she didn't have to leave."

"Then why'd you drive four hours to see me?" he asked, putting a spoon in the fried rice and sliding it toward me.

"Cause I've missed you so much."

"Uh-huh. I've missed you too. Here's your sesame chicken."

"*And?*"

"And your soup."

"Thanks."

"So tell me what it is that's not such a big deal."

"Tanner."

If he'd acted surprised I would have felt better, but he just nodded as if he'd already suspected that's why I'd come.

"What's going on?"

"Nothing, really," I said. "Laci's just worried about him, that's all."

"Why?"

"Have you met Megan?"

"Yeah."

"Did you know that they're living together?"

"No," he said, but again, he didn't seem surprised.

"Well, you know Laci, Mike. She's never been judgmental, but she's just . . . I don't know. I've never seen her so bent outta shape about something before. I don't know what to think. I mean is she making too big of a deal out of this or am I *not* making a big enough deal out of it, or what?"

He took a bite off of an egg roll and chewed it for a minute before answering.

"I've been worried about him too," he finally said.

"You have?"

"Yeah."

"Why?"

He wiped his mouth and put down his napkin.

"It's kinda hard to explain," he said and then he thought for a moment.

"Do you feel like God's been good to you?" he finally asked.

"What kind of a question is that?"

"Just answer it," he said. "I'm going to try to make a point."

"Okay. Yes. God's been good to me."

"Like how?"

"Oh, come on, Mike."

"Just play along," he said, waving his hand for me to continue.

"Fine," I sighed. "Ummm . . . well, obviously I've got Laci and Dorito and Lily, and I've got a great job and I'm back home now, and . . . I don't know. Lots of stuff. Everything."

"What about all the bad things that have happened to you?"

"What do you mean?"

"I mean you're twenty-six years old and you've already had a lot of terrible things happen in your life. How can you say that God's been good to you?"

"Because . . . a lot of good things have come out of them."

"Like what?"

I sighed at him again.

"Like, what good came out of Greg getting killed?"

"A lot of people came to know Christ because of that . . . it's still happening. You know that."

"What about Gabby?"

Gabby was our baby who had died . . . she was stillborn.

"I'm not sure if I know yet what good came from that . . . it definitely brought me closer to God. There's probably a lot more, but I just don't know about it right now."

"What about Laci's miscarriages and her cancer? She almost died."

"We wouldn't have adopted Dorito and Lily if all that hadn't happened."

"But you do agree you've had some bad things happen to you?"

"Of course I do. Everybody's had bad stuff happen to them."

"And yet you *do* feel like God's been good to you . . . like you've been blessed?"

I nodded.

"Well, me too. See, I feel like I've been really blessed and that even the bad things that have happened have resulted in a lot of good. Like my dad . . . you know?"

His dad had died just before Mike entered high school.

"How so?"

I didn't doubt that good had come from it, but he'd never shared it with me.

"Why do you think I'm in med school?" Mike asked.

"I guess I never really thought about it . . ."

"You know how much time I spent in hospitals with him when I was little? That's what got me so interested in medicine in the first place . . . why I became an EMT. You wouldn't believe how much good stuff's already happened just with me being an EMT . . . I can't imagine what it's going to be like once I'm a doctor!"

"By the way," I said. "How'd things go on your call today?"

"Nobody was seriously hurt."

"Good."

"But there've been plenty of times when people haven't been alright," he said. "I've been with a lot of people when they've died . . .

and I've gotten to pray with them and lead some of them to Christ. That's really huge."

"I know . . ."

"And you know what? If Gabby hadn't of died and Laci hadn't of had such a rough time afterwards I never would have met Danica. If I hadn't of become an EMT, Laci probably would have died that night when she was bleeding so bad. If Laci'd died you two wouldn't have led Kelly to Christ. I mean, it's pretty clear that God's been in total control all along."

"Yeah, I already know all that. So what's your point?"

"See," he said, "that's why I'm worried about Tanner. I don't think he feels that way."

"What do you mean?"

"I mean he acts as if he's been . . . *betrayed* or something. Whenever you and I've had bad things happen to us we've known that God's working it to good, but whenever something bad happens to Tanner he doesn't see that."

"What's Tanner had happen to him that's so bad?"

"Well, he lost Greg too . . ."

"Greg was *my* best friend."

"I know," Mike said, "but you weren't the only one that went through something there."

"Okay," I conceded.

"And then his dad just left them one day without even saying goodbye . . . that's gotta be hard."

"I suppose . . ."

"But my point is that *everything* that happens to him – no matter what it is – I don't think he sees the good in it."

"Why?"

"I . . . I don't know. I just know that I've been noticing it more and more."

"Have you tried talking to him?"

"Whenever I do, I just feel like I'm pushing him away. He certainly doesn't want to hear me say anything about God, I can tell you that."

"Are you telling me he's not saved?"

"I don't know."

It was silent for a minute.

"I can't believe this, Mike," I finally said. "I mean, how can we not know if Tanner's saved or not?"

"*You* feel bad? How do you think I feel? He was my best friend!"

"He *was* your best friend? He's not your best friend anymore?"

"I don't know, Dave. Things haven't been good between us in a while . . . I'm not even sure if I'm going to ask him to be in the wedding or not."

"You *have* to . . . he should be your best man . . ."

"I was going to ask you to be my best man," Mike said.

"No . . . it's gotta be Tanner. Don't you see, Mike? He needs us to be his friends right now . . ."

"I don't know, David. I've tried to share my faith with him . . . he doesn't wanna hear it. The Bible says if someone doesn't welcome you you're supposed to shake the dust off your feet . . ."

I could not believe how willing Laci and Mike were to just abandon Tanner. I was *not* going to do that to him.

"It also says that if you're a believer you should stay with the unbelieving because they might be saved," I argued.

Mike burst out laughing.

"They're talking about husbands and wives, you idiot!" he said.

"I know," I said, smiling, "but it's the same principle. I really think we need to be there for him . . . okay?"

Mike hesitated for a moment and then finally nodded.

"Okay."

"So you'll ask him to be your best man?"

"I guess so," he said, "but you're going to be up there too."

50

"Sure I will," I said. "I'll be right there . . . on the other side of Tanner."

On the car ride home I didn't even turn on the radio . . . I just *thought* the whole time.

Many times – especially in Mexico – I had questioned why God had chosen to bless me the way he had. I'd wondered why I wasn't born into a family who was so poor that they had to live in a landfill. Why wasn't I crippled or blind or deaf? Why weren't my children dying from starvation or disease?

Now I thought about Tanner and I wondered how things could be so different for the two of us when we'd grown up together under pretty much the same circumstances.

Like Mike had said, it was fairly easy to look back over things and see clearly that God had been in control all along. Like when He'd brought Greg into my life for example. Now I know (*really I do*) that it wasn't all about me, but anyone would have to admit that one of the main reasons God had moved Greg and his family to Cavendish back when I was twelve was to bring *me* closer to Christ. Okay, and to bring me closer to Laci too, but right now I was thinking about Christ.

How? How did that happen?

I'm not saying I wasn't a Christian before I met Greg, but I was nowhere near the kind of Christian I was by the time Greg was finished with me.

And what exactly was it that Greg had done?

Basically, he'd just always been supportive and he'd always been a good friend.

That's it.

He didn't preach to me, he didn't point out every time I did something wrong. He was just a good friend to me. And in that friendship, I guess I'd seen his relationship with Christ. I'd seen a contentment in him and a peace. I'd seen what he had and I'd seen what I wanted. Isn't that what everybody wants? Whether they admit it or not?

As I drove along I became confident that what I'd told Mike was right . . . we needed to be there for Tanner. Just like Greg had been, I was going to be supportive . . . I was going to be a good friend.

By the time I got home I was feeling a lot better. It felt good to have a game plan.

~ ~ ~

AFTER I GOT home I explained to Laci everything that Mike and I had talked about and everything I'd thought about on the ride home. Just like I figured she would, Laci got right on board with my plan.

It was good knowing that she wasn't going to give me a hard time whenever I wanted to go hunting with Tanner . . . or fishing . . . or skeet shooting. She even started inviting Tanner over for dinner sometimes when Megan was working (which was quite often because Megan was a nurse at the hospital).

The only time Laci ever gave me a hard time was the day I came home from another pheasant hunting trip with Tanner and I told her that I thought we needed to buy a dog.

"A *dog?*" Laci said.

"Yeah. A dog."

"Why?"

"Oh," I said evasively. "It'll be good for the kids."

"Oh, please," she said. "You just want a dog so Tanner can help you train it and you'll have one more excuse to spend time with him."

"So?" (Honestly I don't think she really cared if we got a dog or not.)

"So," she said. "I think buying a dog is going a little overboard. Plus, I know who's going to have to clean up after it when it goes to the bathroom all over the floor."

"They're hardwoods, Laci," I said. "It'll be a snap."

"Yeah," she said. "For YOU!"

"You owe me," I reminded her.

"For *what?*"

"Six Flags," I smiled and she sighed.

We got our name on the list of the same breeder Tanner had bought T.D. from. A litter was due any day and he'd already pre-sold eight, but if more than that were born I would be next on the list. In three days he called and said that eleven had been born and if I wanted a female I could pick her up in time for Christmas.

"What are you going to call her?" Tanner asked.

"I was thinking about *Perro*."

"Why?"

"It's Spanish for 'dog'," I explained.

"You're going to call your dog, '*dog*'?" he asked.

"Yeah," I grinned. "Basically."

"That's the stupidest name I've ever heard of . . . well, except for *Dorito* of course."

"Hey!"

"No offense. Here," he said, ignoring my glare. "You can borrow this book. It's all about training spaniels."

"You're still going to help me, right?"

"Not if you're going to call it *Dog*."

"I'll try to come up with something else," I promised.

~ ~ ~

THE WEEK OF Thanksgiving, Greg's grandmother flew in from Florida to visit Charlotte and Mrs. White. Two days after she arrived we had all three of them over for dinner. Laci had just finished redecorating Lily's bedroom so she showed it off to them before we ate.

"I love it," Charlotte said, running her hands along the border paper.

"I thought you were going to paint the lower half purple," Mrs. White said. "It would have looked good with these flowers here . . ."

"I was going to," Laci sighed, "but David *hates* purple."

"Who hates purple?" Charlotte asked, looking at me.

"*I* hate purple," I said.

"You're so weird."

After dinner we ate cookies in the living room while Dorito set up his Hot Wheels track on the basement stairs and Lily toddled back and forth between our visitors.

"You should come to Florida," Greg's grandmother said when Lily reached her chair.

She lived near the Gulf of Mexico and I'd been down there twice with Greg before he'd died. I smiled at her.

"I'm serious." She looked at Laci. "You two should bring Dorito and Lily to come see me. I hardly ever get any visitors."

Mrs. White was only able to fly down there with Charlotte twice a year – every Christmas break for a week and then for another week over summer vacation. Mr. White had been an only child . . . Greg and Charlotte her only grandchildren.

"You're really serious?" Laci asked her and she nodded.

"When?" I asked.

"Doesn't Dorito get a week off at Easter?"

Laci and I both nodded.

"Well then, you should come down and see me at Easter."

Laci and I both looked at each other and smiled.

"Okay," we said in unison.

"I wanna go!" Charlotte exclaimed.

"No, way," Mrs. White told her.

"Why not?" she cried.

"Because we're flying down less than two months after that and plane tickets don't grow on trees."

Charlotte glared at me.

"I cannot *believe* you get to go and I have to stay here."

"Poor baby," I smiled.

"Oh, shut up."

"We'll really miss you," I assured her. "We'll be thinking about you the *whole* time."

"Thanks a lot."

"We'll need someone to take care of the puppy!" I grinned. "You can do that!"

"And water the plants," Laci suggested.

"And get the mail."

Everybody was laughing except for Charlotte, who narrowed her eyes at me.

"I'm going to get you," she threatened.

"Ooooh!" I said. "I'm so scared."

"Now, now, children," Mrs. White told us. "Be nice."

I smiled, Charlotte scowled, and when I thought no one was looking I stuck my tongue out at her.

~ ~ ~

BASKETBALL SEASON STARTED for Dorito. The kids were barely big enough to dribble the ball, much less throw it into the basket (which was lowered during their games), but they all had a grand time trying and Dorito loved his uniform. He was especially thrilled that he was number five because he was five years old. Actually, I think he was probably six, but when they assign birthdays to orphans without a known birth date they always try to make them as young as possible so they'll be more attractive to prospective parents.

Anyway, basketball practice started and we wound up seeing even *more* of Jordan because he refereed a lot of the little kids' games on Saturday mornings. It was always pretty funny to watch whenever he'd referee one of Dorito's games because Dorito would just stop mid-court and start carrying on a conversation with him. Poor Jordan was too polite to tell Dorito to go on, so he would stand there and nod, acting like he was paying attention to whatever Dorito was saying, all the while trying to keep an eye on the game. Fortunately they didn't even keep score at this age (well, the *parents* did, but officially the league didn't), so it didn't matter too much if Jordan happened to miss a play or two.

One Saturday Charlotte came by during half time and sat down with us. She'd just gotten off of work and remembered that Dorito had a game, so she'd decided to swing by and watch the second half.

"Go, Dorito! Go!" she yelled at the top of her lungs after the starting buzzer sounded. That was a mistake. Dorito turned to where we were sitting, spotted Charlotte and ran over to the bleachers.

"Hi, Charlotte!" he waved as he teammates ran up and down the court behind him.

"Dorito!" Laci said, pointing to the court. "Get out there and play!"

His face clearly said: *Why? Charlotte's here!*

"Go on, Dorito," I nodded.

He looked as if he might cry.

"Go out there and play and I'll take you out to lunch afterwards," Charlotte promised.

Nothing like a bribe to brighten him right up.

"Okay!"

He turned and ran . . . straight up to Jordan.

"Charlotte's here!" we could hear him say, all the way from midcourt. Jordan nodded at him, patted him on the head, and then called a foul on the away team.

Dorito ran back to us after the game and Jordan followed to say hello.

"Good game, buddy," he said, ruffling Dorito's hair.

"Charlotte's taking me out to lunch!"

"That's good," Jordan said. "Have a great time."

"Come with us!" Dorito suggested, his eyes bright at the thought of having both Charlotte *and* Jordan to himself.

"I can't, Dorito," Jordan said, shaking his head. "I've got another game to referee."

"Awww."

Jordan reached over and stroked Lily's cheek and when she turned toward him he smiled at her.

"*Hi, pretty girl,*" he smiled and signed.

She smiled back at him.

"*Bye, bye,*" he spoke and signed. "*I love you.*"

She beamed at him some more.

"See you guys later," he said to the rest of us, waving as he turned and headed back out onto the court.

"He's been learning sign language," I explained to Charlotte.

"I know," she said.

"How do you know?" I asked her.

"Because I see him sitting there with the EC teacher *every day* during lunch learning it."

"Oh," I said.

I don't know exactly *when* I thought he'd been learning it, but I hadn't known he'd been learning it in the cafeteria . . . during lunch.

~ ~ ~

AS SOON AS the school system went on break, Tanner and I made plans to go hunting or ice fishing almost every day. Sometimes we took my dad or Laci's dad, sometimes we took Jordan, and sometimes we took Dorito. It might be just one or any combination of them, but no matter who was with us – almost every morning – we went to *Wilma's* for breakfast before we set out.

I don't know who Wilma was or if she'd ever actually existed, but if she did, she took the term "greasy spoon" to heart. *Wilma's* opened at four in the morning and closed just before noon – serving breakfast to farmers and hunters and fishermen for all the hours in between.

Charlotte worked there every Saturday morning during the school year and on breaks whenever she wasn't visiting her grandmother in Florida. In this way she was both *like* Greg and *not like* Greg. She was *like* him because he'd worked at *Hunter's* – a pizza place just a few steps up from *Wilma's*. She was *not like* him because Greg would never have taken a job that required him to start work at four in the morning . . . he'd barely gotten up on time to get to school every day. Charlotte, on the other hand, said she had a social life and wasn't going to work evenings. Of course, getting up so early in the morning tended to leave Charlotte more than a little on the grumpy side, but that just made her all the more fun to pick on.

Wilma's was attached to a gas station, which not only added to its charm, but made it convenient for us to pick up minnows on our way to the lake. One morning after Christmas, Jordan was with us.

"I'd like a cherry slushy," Jordan told Charlotte when she took our orders.

"We don't have slushy's."

60

"Yes, you do," he said, looking confused and pointing his thumb toward the gas station. There was a door connecting the two. "There's a machine right in there."

"That's not ours . . ."

"Well, can't you get me one from there?"

"No," she said. "If you want one you have to go in there and get it and pay for it in there."

"I'll bet if I wanted one she'd get it for me," I told Jordan.

"I especially wouldn't get one for you," Charlotte said. "If Dorito wanted one I might figure out a way to do it, but that's about it."

"Boy," I said. "For somebody who works for tips you sure aren't very friendly."

"Yeah, right," she said, turning to leave. "Like you're going to tip me."

Actually I *always* tipped her and I tipped her good . . . but I always left it in front of somebody else's plate. All I left in front of mine was a shiny penny . . . I was pretty sure she knew about the other tip though.

While we were waiting for our food, a little girl who was about Dorito's age walked by our table with her father. She was dressed in camouflage from head to toe. Tanner chuckled when he saw her and I made the *Pon, Pon* signal at him. Tanner laughed and shook his head.

"What's that?" Jordan asked.

"What's what?"

"That sign? I don't know that sign."

"That's 'cause it's not a sign," I said.

"Well, what is it then?" he asked.

"Nothing," Tanner said.

"I would tell you," I said, shrugging at Jordan, "but then I'd have to kill you."

He looked at me, puzzled.

"See," I explained, "when we were growing up Greg used to make up these hand signals for stuff, but if he didn't make it up for *you* then he'd never tell you what it meant."

"Like what?"

"Can't tell you," Tanner said. "They were all secret."

"Oh, come on," Jordan said. "Tell me one of 'em."

"I could tell him what this one meant," I said, pinching my thumb and forefinger together and holding it toward Tanner's face.

"And I could pound you through the back of that booth," Tanner replied.

Now Jordan looked really interested.

"Just tell me *one*," he begged.

"Okay," I said. "You know how he and Laci were always growing their hair out to donate it to Locks of Love?"

Jordan nodded.

"Well, he was always bugging me to do it too, so he'd do this," I made a "V" with my fingers and then opened and closed them like scissors, "to try to convince me to do it too."

"So'd you ever do it?" Jordan asked, trying to remember.

"Ha!" Tanner said. "That's a laugh! David was way too worried about what other people thought of him to do something like that. He was mortified just that *Greg* was doing it! You've never seen anybody as uptight as David was in high school."

"I was not uptight!"

"He was more uptight than he is now?" Jordan asked.

"Oh, yeah," Tanner nodded.

"Well *you* try hanging around with the friends I had," I protested. "I had Greg turning into a long-haired, hippie-freak every two years and making hand signals at me all the time and you were like the mutant spawn of the incredible hulk and a garbage disposal. If it hadn't of been for Mike I wouldn't have had any normal friends at all!"

With that, Charlotte appeared and put down three plates in front of Tanner, two in front of Jordan, and one in front of me.

"I can't believe you teach *health*," she muttered, giving Tanner a bottle of ketchup.

"Hey," Tanner whispered after she'd left. "We could make up one about little Ms. Sunshine there!"

Jordan and I laughed and we worked on it over our meal. We weren't as good as Greg, but fortunately Jordan and I had a repertoire of sign language going for us and we taught the sign for "*cheerful*" to Tanner. We chose that one because we knew Charlotte would get the gist of it.

When she came back to our table to give us our bill we all fanned our hands out and passed them in front of our face from our chins to our ears, wiggling our fingers and giving her big, cheesy smiles.

She stood there, glaring at us, and looking for all the world as if she'd really like to make a certain hand signal of her own.

~ ~ ~

JORDAN RANG THE doorbell on Christmas Eve.

"Merry Christmas," he said, handing me a small package.

"Hey," I said. "Thanks. Come on in."

"Hi, Jordan," Laci said, stepping into the living room, followed by Dorito.

"Hi, Laci," he said, handing her a bag with more presents in it.

"You didn't have to get us anything," Laci said.

"Yes, I did," he argued. "David won't take any money for tutoring me . . . my mom and I wanted to thank you somehow."

"Just pitch a no-hitter for me at your first college game," I said and he smiled.

Then I opened my present.

"Thanks, Jordan!" I said. He'd gotten me a flash drive with a ton of songs on it.

"That's for the next road trip our youth group goes on," he grinned. Then he assured me: "Don't worry . . . I paid for 'em before I downloaded 'em."

Laci and Dorito opened their presents while I went and retrieved one for Jordan from under the tree.

Jordan opened it and grinned again. It was a little miniature basketball goal like the one in my office.

"*Wow*, David," Laci said when she saw it. "You really went all out, didn't you? What'd that set you back? Three bucks?"

"It's the thought that counts," I told her.

"Actually, I love it," Jordan said. "And I'm afraid I'll probably get a lot of use out of it . . ."

"Okay," Laci said doubtfully, looking at his smile. "As long as you're happy."

The doorbell rang again and we opened it to find Tanner.

"Hi, Tanner," Laci said, giving him a hug. "Come on in."

64

Dorito bounded up in front of Tanner and Tanner opened his arms wide. Then Dorito hauled his fist back and slugged Tanner in the stomach as hard as he could.

"*DORITO!*" Laci yelled.

"It's okay," I assured her. "It's just something they do."

"So it's okay for him to punch people?"

"No," I replied, shaking my head. "Just Tanner."

"Yeah," Dorito agreed. "I only get to hit Tanner."

"I don't think we need to be teaching him that it's okay to be *hitting* people . . ."

"Come on, Laci," I said. "Haven't you ever felt like smacking Tanner?"

She looked at me, still uncertain and I tilted my head at her.

"I guess you're right," she finally smiled, nodding at Dorito. "Go ahead and hit him as hard as you want."

Dorito took a few more swings and then Tanner scooped him up and held him over his shoulder.

Tanner glanced at me.

"I, ummm, you know," he said, nodding his head across the street. He was letting me know that he'd dropped our new puppy off with his mom.

"Gotcha," I said, giving him the thumbs up.

"What?" Dorito asked, looking at me up upside down.

"Nothing," I said.

"It's about a Christmas present, isn't it?"

"Nope," Tanner shook his head and flipped Dorito back onto the floor. "I happen to know that you aren't getting any Christmas presents this year."

"Tell me! Tell me! Tell me!" Dorito was bouncing up and down, tugging on Tanner's arm.

"Boy," Jordan said. "Tomorrow's gonna be fun at your house."

Tanner and I decided to go ice fishing the day after Christmas. I told him all about the puppy and how excited the kids had been as we drove along.

"Hoover?" Tanner asked, incredulous. "You named her *Hoover?*"

"It's your brother's fault . . ." I said. Jordan had wanted to make sure Lily knew the sign for "dog" before Christmas morning so he'd been reading her a book all about a dog that sucked up food like a vacuum. Somehow Dorito had gotten his heart set on naming her Hoover.

"And you couldn't talk him out of it?"

"Not really," I said.

"Your family's got a real issue with names . . . you know that?"

"Didn't you just miss our turn?" I asked.

"No . . ."

"Aren't we going to Cross Lake?"

"Naw," he said. "I thought we'd go to Makasoi."

"*Why?*" Cross Lake was about twenty minutes closer, was bigger, and it had better access.

"Cross Lake's always too crowded. I'd rather go to Makasoi . . ."

"Whatever," I said. "You're driving."

We pulled into a convenience store and went in for some drinks and food for the day. We were standing in line to pay when Tanner noticed two Latino men talking near the door.

"What are they saying?" Tanner whispered.

"Who?"

"Those guys over there . . . what are they saying?"

I tuned in.

"*Hola, hombre, tus dientes son muy blancos.*"

"*Gracias.*"

"*¿Como los pones tan blancos?*"

"*Realmente, nada.*"

"*¿No usas un tratamiento de blanqueador ni nada?*"

"*No, los cepillo muy bien dos veces al dia . . . trato de ir al dentista dos veces al año.*"

"*Hombre, son bien blancos.*"

"*Gracias.*"

"They're talking about teeth," I said quietly.

"Teeth?"

"Yeah. The guy in the black coat wants to know what the other guy does to get his teeth so white."

"You're serious?" he asked. "They're talking about *teeth?*"

"Yeah. Why?"

"I don't know," Tanner said, looking disappointed. "It just sounded a whole lot more interesting than that."

"Mike called me last night," Tanner said a few days later. We were getting ready to go hunting, but first he was fixing a gutter on his mom's house that had come down in our last ice storm.

"What's going on with him?" I asked.

"Nothing, I guess." He seemed to hesitate and he also seemed to be avoiding my eyes, but of course he was up on a ladder.

Finally he said, "He asked me if I'd be his best man."

Oh, I got it. He was afraid my feelings were going to be hurt because Mike had asked him and not me.

"Did you tell him 'no'?" I laughed.

Tanner looked down at me, puzzled.

"Why would I tell him 'no'?"

"'Cause they don't make tuxes in your size."

"Very funny." He adjusted the gutter with one hand. "No . . . I told him I'd do it, but I was kind of surprised that he asked me."

"How come?"

"Oh, I don't know," he shrugged, taking a nail out of his mouth. "We just haven't been hanging out all that much anymore."

67

"Well," I said. "He does live four hours away . . ."

"I suppose," Tanner agreed.

"But you guys have always been best friends — that doesn't change just because you don't see each other very often."

"I suppose," he said again.

"He asked me to be an usher," I told him. "It'll be just like when we were little . . . all three of us together again. It'll be great."

"Yeah," Tanner finally smiled and looked down at me, nodding. "It'll be great."

~ ~ ~

ONE OF THE many good things about living in Cavendish again was that we almost always had someone to babysit the kids. We had my parents, Laci's parents, my sister, Mrs. White, Charlotte and Jordan. We usually asked Charlotte first because she always let us pay her. None of the others would – not even Jordan. He was forever going on about how he wanted to pay me back for all the help I was giving him in math.

Charlotte came over one Saturday in January to babysit because Laci and I were going to a workday at the church. It had snowed hard the night before and Dorito was beside himself with excitement.

"Can we go out now?" he was begging Charlotte as we left. "Can we go out now?"

"Is it okay if Lydia comes over later?" she asked us, holding up a finger to quiet Dorito.

"Sure it is," Laci told her.

"Can we go out now? Can we go out now?"

"Have fun," I smiled at her and closed the door.

When we got home Lydia and Charlotte were playing in the snow with Lily and Dorito and about a half of a dozen neighborhood kids were sledding on our hill.

"We've got such a great yard," I told Laci and she grinned at me. She took Lily inside to lay her down for a nap and pretty soon Dorito and I were having a snowball fight against Lydia and Charlotte. We were hiding behind a snow fort that someone had started while we were gone, trying to make snowballs, when all of a sudden . . .

Wham!

Before I knew what had hit me, I was sprawled face down in the snow, barely able to breath. There was only one person who was big enough to do that to me and he'd *been* doing that to me ever since we were about ten years old.

"*GET OFF ME, TANNER!*" I hollered, but of course he couldn't understand what I was saying because my face was full of snow, so he just sat on me a little harder. I hollered a few more times and he must have decided that I was saying 'Uncle' (which I knew was what he wanted to hear) because he finally let me up.

"I'm gonna *kill* you, Tanner," I said, wiping snow out of my eyes.

"You and what army?" he grinned.

As if in reply Jordan came sailing out of nowhere and knocked him to the ground and then Lydia and Charlotte each sat on one of his arms while Jordan and I pinned down his legs. Dorito started stuffing fistfuls of snow down the neck of his coat, but nowhere near enough as far as I was concerned.

Tanner laughed for a minute, but once he decided that he'd had enough he just raised his arm and lifted Lydia right off the ground. Charlotte screamed when she saw that happen and abandoned her post almost as fast as Jordan and I did.

We all scattered and I wound up near the front porch just as Laci came out with the baby monitor.

"She settle down?" I asked.

"Yeah," Laci nodded, sitting on the top step. I climbed the steps and sat down next to her, putting my arm around her as we watched everyone play in the snow. Tanner grabbed Charlotte and pinned her down while Dorito and Jordan stuffed snow down her hood.

"I don't know why Tanner doesn't want kids," Laci said quietly. "He's just a big kid himself."

Charlotte finally got free and chased Jordan across the yard with a fist full of snow and I thought about the two of them . . . Charlotte and Jordan.

Four years earlier Charlotte had come down to Mexico on a mission trip. At the time she'd told me that she *despised* Jordan . . . absolutely couldn't stand him. I didn't understand why she let him make her so upset and I asked her why she didn't just ignore him. After some prodding she'd finally confessed that God had told her that she and Jordan were going to be together one day . . . something she desperately didn't want to believe at the time.

Now I watched as they chased each other, laughing, and throwing snow at each other.

"Hey," I said to Laci. "Remember that snow day when we all wound up at Greg's house?"

"When his grandmother was there?"

"Yeah."

"What about it?"

"Remember how we got invited to stay for lasagna?"

"I'm not making lasagna," Laci said.

"*Why not?*"

"Well, for one thing it takes too long and for another thing I don't have the ingredients."

"Oh," I sighed.

"I *will* order pizza though," she said, smiling.

"Good enough."

We walked into the yard.

"Where's Lydia?" Laci asked, looking around.

"She had to go," Charlotte said.

"Oh. I wish I'd caught her . . . I was going to invite everyone to stay for pizza. Do you want to stay?"

"Thanks, but I can't."

"How come?" I asked, immediately disappointed.

"I've got a date," she answered.

"What about you, Jordan?" Laci asked.

"Yeah, thanks," he said, nodding. She turned to go inside when Tanner called out to her.

"What about me? Aren't you going to invite me?"

"I kind of figured it was a given that you'd stay," Laci said, glancing back at him. "I've never known you to turn down a meal."

Depending on how late it was and what the weather was like, I usually either walked or drove Charlotte home after she babysat for us. Even though the pizza was going to arrive soon, I decided I'd walk her home that night.

"What?" she asked after we'd reached the sidewalk.

"What, what?" I said.

She looked at me and smiled.

"Well, obviously you want to talk to me about something or you would have driven me home."

"I'm that predictable?" I asked.

"Pretty much," she said. "Let me guess. You want to stay and meet my date."

"No," I said. "I want to stay and *glare* at your date . . . or maybe go on your date with you and make sure he stays in line."

"This isn't my first date, David," she said, laughing. "I'm almost seventeen."

"You make me feel so old."

"You are old."

"Thanks a lot."

She put her arm around my waist and gave me a quick squeeze.

"What else?" she asked.

"Am I really *that* predictable?"

She gave me a sideways glance and raised her eyebrow at me.

"I was just watching you and Jordan today," I said, "and I was thinking about what you told me down in Mexico, that's all."

"I can't believe you even remember that," she said, shaking her head and laughing lightly. "Just forget about it."

"But Charlotte," I protested. "You said that-"

"I was in the *seventh* grade, David."

"So?"

"So it was a mistake. It's no big deal."

"What do you mean, a mistake? God doesn't make mistakes . . ."

"No," she said, shaking her head. "I don't mean *God* made a mistake . . . I mean *I* did. I don't think God really told me that."

"Why not?"

"I don't know," she shrugged. "I just think I made a mistake, that's all. Sometimes people make mistakes."

We walked along silently for a minute and then she bumped her shoulder against mine.

"What's wrong now?" she asked.

"Your brother would do a much better job at this than me."

"First of all, you're making too big of a deal out of everything, *as usual*, and second of all," she put her arm around my waist again, "you do a great job."

I put my arm around her shoulder and squeezed.

"Not as good as Greg," I said.

"I'm gonna be so sore tomorrow," I groaned, rubbing my shoulder. I picked up another piece of pizza and looked at Laci. "This is why we need to get a hot tub off of the deck. Think how good it would feel to go sit out there after dinner."

"What you *need*," Tanner said, "is to get some exercise."

"What makes you think I don't exercise?"

"Do you exercise?"

"Well–" I began.

"No," Laci interjected.

"For your information, Laci, I've been thinking about joining the Y."

"You've been *thinking* about it?" Tanner laughed and I nodded. "*Thinking* about it's not going to get you in shape."

"I'm in great shape."

"Oh *really?*" He laughed again. "You wanna go play racquetball next Saturday?"

"I think I'll pass."

"Oh, come on. Why not?"

I glanced at Jordan. He was signing to me with a slight smile on his face.

I can teach you . . .

I looked at Tanner again who was sitting there with a smug look on his face, then I glanced back at Jordan one more time.

I can help you beat him . . .

"Yeah, okay," I said, nodding at Tanner. "Why not?"

On Monday we bought a family membership to the Y and after dinner Laci took the kids to free swim while Jordan taught me how to play.

Jordan, who was normally so quiet, was suddenly in his element. I think he really enjoyed being the one with all the answers for a change.

"Try to get it over here as much as possible," he said, tapping the back left corner with his racket. "Tanner can hardly ever get it off this wall."

"Okay . . ."

"And if you even *think* his serve's gonna hit the back wall," Jordan said, "just let it go. He whacks it as hard as he can when he's playing and a lot of time he forgets to tone it down when he's serving."

"Okay . . ."

74

"Speaking of which . . . if he hits you with the ball it's gonna hurt."

"Great."

He spent a lot of time helping me practice my serve.

"Pretend like you've got a rolled up newspaper under this arm," he said. "You're bringing your elbow out too far from your body."

I tried it again.

"How was that?"

"It can't go in front of this line on the serve, remember?"

"Why not?"

"That's the rule."

"Well that's a stupid rule," I muttered.

"What's the matter? I thought you *liked* rules."

"Math is different," I said. "The rules in math make sense."

He just laughed at me.

"Now look," he said a little later. "He's got power and he's a lot more agile than he looks. The only way you're going to beat him is if you're more accurate than he is."

"Gee, Jordan. *Thanks.*"

"Well," he said, "you know what I mean."

"Sadly, yes, I'm afraid I do. I'm gonna get creamed."

"Not necessarily," he said. "It's all about physics. This is where all those angles of reflection and everything you've got cluttering up your head are going to come in handy."

"I can't believe you just used the term 'angles of reflection' in the right context . . ." I said in mock astonishment.

"How's that?" he asked, grinning. "That they're cluttering up your head?"

"Very funny."

After we'd played for over an hour we decided to quit for the night.

"If you think you were sore after a snowball fight," Jordan warned, "just wait until tomorrow."

"Great."

I wanted to swim some laps in the pool before my muscles seized up on me. I really *had* been thinking about joining the Y long before my conversation with Tanner. I'd been hoping that if I could swim three or four times a week maybe I could get my times down to where they'd been in college. *Maybe . . .*

"You haven't been here since they renovated?" Jordan asked when he had to show me where the new locker rooms were.

"Nope."

We got to the men's locker room.

"Go out those doors," he said, pointing past the showers. "They'll take you right up to the pool."

"Where are you going?" I asked him.

"Indoor batting cage," he grinned and took off.

I changed into my suit, showered, and went through the doors Jordan had pointed to earlier. The pool was all new too and at the far end of it there was . . . *a giant hot tub*.

"How'd that go?" Laci asked when I walked up to her and the kids at the shallow end.

"I'm pretty much not going to be able to move in the morning."

She laughed. "Are you gonna do laps?"

"Well," I said, glancing over at the hot tub, "I was planning to, but . . ."

"Dorito's been dying to go over there," she smiled, "but I can't take him because Lily's too little."

That was all I needed to hear.

"This is so cool!" Dorito said a few minutes later as he paddled around. "We should get one of these for our back yard!"

"You know what?" I said. "That's *exactly* what I've been telling Mommy."

76

We went to the Y every evening that week. Jordan assured me that he'd be okay missing a week of tutoring and by Friday night I was . . . well, I wasn't horrible. Neither Jordan nor I deluded ourselves into thinking I might actually beat Tanner, but we were hoping I could at least give him a run for his money. My goal was to score at least eight or nine points on him.

The next afternoon my phone rang as I was pulling in the driveway.

"How'd it go?" Jordan asked. He must have been watching for my car.

"My best game I scored eleven."

"Are you serious?"

"Yup."

"That's great! Was he surprised?"

"I think so," I said. "He wouldn't admit it, but I don't think he was expecting me to ever get that many on him."

"I'll bet you could beat him in a few more weeks if we keep practicing!"

"You're gonna fall behind in math," I warned.

"We'll do math one day and racquetball the next . . ."

I couldn't pass up the chance to finally beat Tanner at something.

"Okay," I said. "Deal."

About ten days later we were working on my serve again. Jordan had been right about Tanner not being able to get them off the back left wall and I had scored most of my points on him when I was able to get the ball there on my serve.

"Good," Jordan said when I sent one past him. I turned around to smile and I saw Tanner's face peering at us through the little square window.

"Uh-oh," I said, nodding toward the door. "I think we're busted."

Tanner stepped in shaking his head.

"Well, well, well," he said. "What have we here?"

"I'm helping Jordan with his geometry."

"Oh, really?"

"Uh-huh. I was just explaining to him how this room's a good example of a rectangular prism . . ."

We both glanced at Jordan who was innocently staring up at the ceiling, trying very hard not to smile.

"You think you're pretty smart, don't you?" he asked, turning back to me.

"Compared to who? You?"

He narrowed his eyes and then smiled.

"Feel like playing cutthroat?"

"Cutthroat?"

"I'm sure my little brother here can explain all the rules to you while I go get my racket," he said, turning to leave. "And I'm not going to go easy on you this time."

He'd been going easy on me last time?

He closed the door and I looked at Jordan.

"Cutthroat?" I asked again.

"Yeah," Jordan said. "It's for three people . . ."

"He's gonna whip our butts isn't he?"

"Probably," Jordan grinned.

Our first game wasn't too bad . . . Tanner won with fifteen, Jordan had thirteen, and I got nine. But Tanner accused Jordan of going easy on me whenever it was my serve, so Jordan played harder for our second game. I'm not even going to tell you the score of that one.

78

"Don't feel too bad, Davey," Tanner said, clapping me on the shoulder afterwards. "I'll bet you can still beat me in chess."

"I'll bet *Dorito* can beat you in chess," I said. My hands were on my knees and I was still trying to catch my breath.

Jordan went off to the batting cage, but Tanner followed me to the pool. When he saw Dorito paddling around a few feet from Laci and Lily he started charging across the cement floor.

"Aaaaaarrrrrrrrrrrgggggggghhhhh!" he called at the top of his lungs and Dorito whirled around just in time to see Tanner's feet leaving the edge of the pool. Dorito's eyes got wide and then he screamed in delight as Tanner made a cannonball and landed about a foot from him. The lifeguard blew her whistle at Tanner.

Tanner waved apologetically to the lifeguard and then he picked Dorito up and tossed him about three yards through the air. Dorito came up squealing and giggling, having the time of his life. The lifeguard blew her whistle at Tanner again.

~ ~ ~

DESPITE THE FACT that we had a plethora of babysitters at our disposal, Laci hardly ever managed to make it to youth group. She did manage, however, to come up with all sorts of suggestions about things she thought "*we*" should do with the youth group. One of the things Laci suggested was that the youth group go to a True Love Waits conference. Actually she didn't just suggest it, she made reservations.

Even though she was doing a great job of being supportive and being a good friend to Tanner, she never missed an opportunity to remind *me* of the many benefits of abstinence before marriage. I think what she really wanted was to hear me say that I agreed with her . . . that people should wait until they get married.

She never got to hear me say it though. It wasn't so much that I actually *disagreed* with her as it was that I didn't want to feel as if I were judging Tanner. Judging was not being supportive . . . it wasn't being a good friend.

"You know," she said one day, "this message is going to be really good for the kids to hear."

"Uh-huh."

"It's not just about waiting until you get married. They need to learn that you have to keep your spirit pure and your thoughts pure . . . and that's something they're going to have to do for their entire lives.

"Uh-huh."

"That doesn't all end just because you get married – it's a different kind of battle, but it's still a battle."

That made me perk up my ears.

"Are you trying to tell me something, Laci? Is there some hot bag-boy at the grocery store that you're having a hard time keeping your mind off of?"

She laughed.

"I'm just saying that I think this conference is going to be really good for the kids."

"Uh-huh."

Jordan signed up for the conference.

Just Jordan.

I wound up spending the entire day taking him all by myself.

"You planned this, didn't you?" I asked Laci before I left.

"Yeah, right," she said, kissing me goodbye. "Have a good time."

"Oh, I'm sure I will. I'll probably come back a changed man."

She smiled at me.

"I'm serious, Laci. You're going to be sorry. I'm going to come back thinking you and I'd better start abstaining or something."

She laughed. "I'm willing to take my chances."

"Thanks a lot."

Jordan was waiting for me on his front porch. When he saw me come out the front door he stood up and hollered into his house and then he met me in the driveway. His mom came over and started going on and on about how great his math grades were now and thanking me for everything I was doing for him.

"Just trying to pay you back for that lamp," I said.

"It was priceless . . . irreplaceable. You'll never be able to pay me back."

"I'm going to keep trying though," I said, climbing into the car. She smiled at me and we pulled out of the driveway.

"What lamp?" Jordan asked.

"Oh, some piece of junk I accidentally broke when I was about eleven."

"Was it really irreplaceable?"

"No," I said. "She just likes to tease me . . . I think."

"Probably," he assured me. "She wouldn't dare have had anything priceless around the house with the three of us."

"I can imagine," I said. "It's bad enough with just Dorito and Lily."

"Did you bring the music?" he asked.

"Of course," I said, holding the flash drive that he had given me for Christmas out to him. He took it from me and plugged it in.

We rode along and listened for a few minutes.

"I'm sorry you're having to drive all this way just for me," he said after a while. "If I'd known ahead of time that I was going to be the only one to sign up I wouldn't have wasted your time."

"You're not wasting my time," I said. "I don't mind one bit."

"Well, anyway . . . thanks."

"No problem. Besides, I think Laci would have been pretty upset if we weren't going."

"Why's that?"

"Oh, nothing . . . it's a long story."

One I'm not going to get into with Tanner's little brother.

"Oh."

"Did you bring your math?"

"Yeah."

"Good," I said. "It's going to be about a two hour drive."

"I'm five sections ahead of the class though . . . I don't know how much further ahead I should get. I'm afraid I'm going to forget everything before she gets to it."

"Why are we *five* sections ahead?"

"Because she missed three days this week and we had a sub who didn't make us do anything."

"Oh, brother."

The conference was better than I thought it would be – not that I was ever going to admit that to Laci. Just like Laci had said, they talked to the kids about not only how important it was to remain abstinent until marriage, but also how important it was to keep their spirits pure and their thoughts pure.

They were reminded that Jesus had said, "You have heard that it was said, 'Do not commit adultery'. But I tell you that anyone who looks at a woman lustfully has already committed adultery with her in his heart."

By Jesus' definition, being sexually pure meant not even dwelling on sexual thoughts about someone other than your spouse. They were also told that during the afternoon session, they would have an opportunity to sign commitment cards and make a pledge to remain sexually pure.

We broke for lunch and Jordan and I went to a sub shop on the edge of campus.

"Can I ask you something?" Jordan wanted to know after we'd sat down.

"Sure."

"I mean it's kind of personal so you don't have to tell me if you don't want to . . ."

"What?"

"Did you and Laci, ummm . . . you know?"

"Huh?" (Sometimes it took me a while.)

"Did you wait?"

"Oh."

"You don't have to tell me," he said again quickly.

"No, it's okay," I said. "We waited, but it was kind of different with me and Laci."

"Different?"

"Well, yeah. You probably don't remember that much about me and Laci when we were dating, do you?"

"I remember when Laci babysat me one time and you came over and helped her."

"That was probably not too long before Greg died," I said. "Laci and I dated for like five or six months just before he got killed."

"Okay."

"Well, we started dating in the summer and we were just getting to really know each other . . . I mean we'd *known* each other forever, but you know what I mean. Plus it was our senior year and Greg and I were up to our necks in AP Physics and calculus and we had soccer and youth group on top of everything else and it seemed like I barely had time to breathe."

"Laci and I just never got to that point in our relationship where we needed to make a decision about it and we broke up right before Christmas."

"You broke up?"

"I guess we didn't really 'break up', we just kind of quit seeing each other."

"Why?"

"I just . . . I had a really hard time after Greg died. I pushed everybody away and then I came here to State and Laci went off to Collins and then when we finally did get back together again it was about five months before we were supposed to graduate. We were living four hours apart from each other and there was hardly time to even plan our wedding before we moved to Mexico. It was just kind of obvious that we were going to wait. We never really even thought about it."

Okay – maybe I'd thought *about it . . .*

"Oh."

84

"But . . . I mean, trust me. If we'd thought about it or talked about it or whatever, I'm pretty sure that we still would have waited."

"Really?"

An image of Laci yelling at me about Tanner and Megan living together flashed through my mind.

"Yeah," I said, laughing. "I'm pretty confident that Laci would have seen to it that we waited."

Jordan smiled.

"But that's what I meant when I said it was different with us. I don't know . . . I'm sure it would have been a lot harder if we hadn't been going through all that other stuff."

Jordan nodded at me.

"It's not just about waiting until you get married. You have to keep your spirit pure and your thoughts pure. That's something you're going to have to do for your entire life."

Did I just say that?

"It doesn't all end just because you get married . . . it's a different kind of battle, but it's still a battle."

Man, I sounded just like Laci. I *hated* it when that happened.

Jordan was quiet for a few moments.

"I think I'm going to take that pledge this afternoon," Jordan finally said.

"Really?"

"Uh-huh."

"You don't have to just because of what I said . . ."

That's real good, David. Why don't you try to talk him out of it?

"No," he said. "I think it's what God wants me to do. I've really, really been trying to do what God wants me to do . . . you know what I mean?"

"Yeah. I know what you mean."

"Thanks for talking to me. Tanner doesn't ever talk to me like you do. Thanks."

"No problem."

It was quiet for a moment until he finally spoke again.

"Sometimes I worry about Tanner," he said. "You know what I mean?"

"Yeah," I said again. "I know what you mean."

I really liked Jordan. I think what I liked most about him was that he didn't care what anybody else thought of him. As long as he thought he was doing what God wanted him to do it didn't matter to him what other people might say. Greg had been the same way.

The reason Greg had always grown his hair out and donated it to Locks of Love was because when he'd moved to town he'd found out that's what Laci had been doing ever since she was a little girl. He'd thought it was a great idea – so he'd started doing it too. Like Tanner had told Jordan, I'd been absolutely mortified, but Greg didn't worry about it at all. I don't think he ever got teased for having long hair, but even if he *had* he wouldn't have let that stop him. Greg had also bowed his head every day and prayed in the cafeteria at school too. Not a lot of kids did that.

Likewise, Jordan did what he thought was right. If the other kids weren't listening to Christian music he'd just stick his earphones in and ignore them. And most kids don't sit in the cafeteria with an E.C. teacher learning sign language during lunch.

Granted we didn't *know* anyone at the conference, but I had a feeling that if every person Jordan had known was there he still would have taken that pledge. That's just the kind of person that he was.

With only about ten minutes left in our return trip home, Jordan asked if he could skip ahead to a song he said he really wanted to hear. He must have spent a fortune on all those songs he'd bought me . . . we hadn't even come close to listening to all of them.

"Go ahead," I answered and he punched away at the buttons.

The song he'd wanted to hear turned out to be Casting Crowns' *Every Man* – the same song I'd been so glad to hear when we'd been riding to Six Flags just before that girl named Stephanie had changed the station. I must have given Jordan a funny look when I realized what song it was.

"What?" he asked.

"Nothing," I said. "I'm just surprised that this is the one you wanted to hear, that's all."

"I know it's kinda old," he apologized. "But it's one of my favorites."

I really liked Jordan.

"Of course you do," Laci said when I told her that.

"What's that supposed to mean?"

"I mean he's *just* like you! Of course you like him."

"What are you talking about? He's not like me."

"He's practically a little 'mini-Dave'!"

"No, he's not!"

"Yes, he is! How can you *not* see that? You're two of the most reserved people I've ever met in my entire life! You're both so quiet around people you don't know and you've both got the same dry sense of humor . . ."

I guess I could see some similarities if I looked at it that way; but there was something very different about Jordan – something that I couldn't quite put my finger on.

I spent the next few weeks trying to figure out what it was.

As Laci had said, I wasn't a terribly social person, and neither was Jordan, but I'd always had friends . . . *close* friends.

Jordan, on the other hand, didn't seem to. Instead he had *acquaintances* . . . people he knew from school or guys he played baseball with or something like that. He was friendly with them and everybody seemed to like him well enough, but he didn't seem to have any real *friends*. I never heard him talk about anybody and I never saw him doing anything with other people. As a matter of fact, he spent most of his free time with me, doing math.

I mean what kind of kid spends all of his free time doing *math?*

Okay. I realize that coming from me that probably sounds like a strange question since I'd spent plenty of time doing math when I was his age, but that was a totally different situation.

For one thing, I'd always *enjoyed* math and I was good at it. Jordan (on the other hand) hated math and struggled with it all the time. Why would he work so hard in math? Was it because he had to make a 'C' or better in order to stay on the baseball team? Was it because he wanted good enough grades to get into college? I didn't think so; he could have done that just by coming over once or twice a week. He didn't have to come over *every* day and work for two hours each night.

Another reason it was different was because of Greg. Greg had set some pretty high goals for himself: he'd wanted to get into one of the best engineering schools in the country and become an engineer. He *had* to work hard in math if he wanted to succeed and he'd sucked me right in with him. It became something we did together . . . for us it was almost social. On the surface that may sound weird, but if you think about it, you tend to find ways to spend as much time as you can with the people that you like best.

And there it was.

Jordan was trying to find ways to spend time with me.

It didn't have anything to do with math and it didn't have anything to do with youth group.

It had to do with the fact that Jordan acted as if I was the best (or only) friend that he had.

~ ~ ~

JORDAN NEEDS SOME friends his own age," I told Laci.

"I'm sure he has friends his own age."

"Like who?"

"Well, I don't know. I don't know who his friends are, but I'm sure he has some."

"If he had friends don't you think we'd know about them? He's over here *all the time*. Don't you think he'd talk about 'em every now and then and we'd know their names?"

"What are you saying?"

"I'm saying I don't think it's good for a sixteen-year-old kid to be hanging around at his youth group leader's house all the time."

"You were over at the White's all the time," she argued.

"To see Greg!" I protested. "I wasn't over there to visit with Mr. or Mrs. White or to play with Charlotte!"

She thought for a moment.

"But you're helping Jordan with his math . . ."

"He doesn't need *that* much help, Laci. Not even *you* needed that much help."

"I'll have you know that I didn't need much help at all – I was just looking for an excuse to be with you."

"And I think Jordan's just looking for an excuse to hang out over here because he doesn't have any friends."

"Well, he probably considers you to be his friend."

"I *know* he does . . . that's what I'm saying. He needs friends his own age. He doesn't need to be friends with someone who's ten years older than him and who has a wife and kids."

"I wonder why he doesn't have any friends his own age?"

I'd been wondering the same thing and I thought I'd figured it out.

90

"Jordan's not your typical teenager," I said. "I mean, I think it's pretty unusual for someone his age to be as mature as he is when it comes to his relationship with God."

"We were."

"We were typical? Come on, Laci. Where'd we go over our spring breaks?"

"The youth rallies in Chicago . . ."

"Where do most kids go over their spring breaks?"

She looked at me.

"There are lots of kids out there who are like we were," she said. "They might not all be going to youth rallies over spring break, but they're not all spending their time getting drunk at Daytona Beach either."

"I know, but what I'm saying is that Jordan doesn't know any of the kids who are like we were."

"He knows all the kids in youth group."

"Laci! Every kid in that youth group *except for Jordan* is there because their parents are making them be there. Unless we're doing something fun like going to Six Flags or something they have to be dragged there. I'm not saying that they're bad kids or that they don't love God, but I am saying that they're just not where Jordan is right now."

"Okay," she conceded. "I can see that."

"And I think he wants to be around someone else who's got a strong relationship with Christ . . . he wants to be able to talk to someone . . . like you and Greg and I were able to do."

"That's understandable," she agreed.

"So we've got to find him someone," I said. "Someone else besides me . . . someone his *own age*."

"How in the world are we going to do that?"

"Simple," I said, smiling at her because I'd already figured that out too. "I'm going to call Ashlyn."

~ ~ ~

"WHAT'S WRONG?" ASHLYN asked.

"Do you always answer the phone like that?"

"Only when I know it's you," she said. "You never call me unless something's wrong. So what's wrong?"

"Nothing's *wrong*," I said. "Well, not really . . ."

"I knew it."

"I just need some help with this youth group you got me roped into," I said.

"How did *I* get you roped into it?"

"I'm not sure," I admitted. "All I know is that we invited you over for some lasagna and the next thing I know I'm in charge of the youth group at a church I don't even belong to."

She laughed.

"So how can I help?"

"You wanna get together for lunch tomorrow? Laci'll watch Amelia for you . . ."

"Sure," she said.

"Where do you want to go?"

"Ummm . . . Mexican's always good unless you've had enough Mexican to last you a lifetime."

"Mexican's fine," I said. "It's not the same here anyway."

We met at eleven-thirty to avoid the lunch crowd.

"Was Dorito excited to see Amelia?" I asked as we waited to be seated. I'd been in town mailing some documents when she'd dropped her daughter off at our house.

"Oh yeah," she nodded.

"When are you going to give us a playmate for Lily?" I teased.

92

"We're trying."

"Seriously?"

"Yep," she smiled.

I smiled back at her as a waiter put a basket of chips and a bowl of salsa down in front of us.

"I'm starving," Ashlyn said, grabbing a chip. "If I didn't know better, I'd think I was pregnant right now."

"This isn't going to be like eating with Tanner, is it?"

"I'll bet I could give him a run for his money."

After another waiter came by and took our order, Ashlyn asked me, "So, what's up?"

"Well," I began, "our youth group is the pits and I need help."

"The pits how?"

"I don't know," I said. "Nobody likes going to youth group . . . *I* don't even like going to youth group."

"So you want some ideas?"

"No," I said. "It's more than that. They're just not . . . I don't know. It's just a bad mix of kids. They form about three little cliques and poor Jordan's in a clique all by himself. They don't have good relationships with each other, you know? Remember how much fun we all had when we were in youth group together? That never happens with these kids . . . *never.*"

"Well," she said, "Mr. White was a really good leader."

"Thank you, Ashlyn," I sighed. "I'm well aware that I'm failing miserably."

"No, you're not," she laughed. "I'm just kidding. I had a group like that three years ago."

"Really?"

"Yep," she nodded.

"So what do I do?"

"You just get through the end of the year. It'll be better next year."

"Oh, come on, Ashlyn," I said. "I don't want to do that."

"Well, what else *can* you do?" she asked. "You can't *make* them have fun with each other."

"I had an idea . . ."

"Oh no," she said and I grinned.

By the time lunch was over we'd laid the foundation for the greatest Easter pageant ever . . . and our two youth groups were going to collaborate on it for the next ten weeks.

~ ~ ~

ALTHOUGH MOST OF the time I could work from home, sometimes my job required me to travel to areas that had been hit by earthquakes to inspect minimally impacted buildings for structural damage. We'd gotten the youth groups together for play practice *one time* when I got sent away for what turned out to be three weeks.

"I'm really sorry, Ashlyn," I said when I called to tell her I'd be gone for a while. "Laci's gonna try to help you while I'm gone."

"*Try?*"

"Yeah," I said. "You'll see."

Actually, Laci managed to make it to every meeting while I was gone. Apparently spending more time with Ashlyn was a better incentive for finding a babysitter than spending more time with *me* was.

"Well you're home *all the time*," she said when I called from California and accused her of that.

"So basically you like it when I go to youth group by myself because it gives you a chance to be away from me."

"I didn't say that!"

"You didn't have to," I teased. "I bet you're having the time of your life with me halfway across the country."

"Oh, stop it."

Laci said that putting our youth groups together was working out fantastic. The kids already knew each other because they went to high school together and the chemistry among them was different once they all got together. Ashlyn was so impressed with the way they interacted that she told Laci we should keep meeting jointly even after the play was over. I told Laci to tell Ashlyn that she had a deal.

"Guess what happened today?" I asked.

"What?"

"I was talking to this guy who works out of Oregon and he started complaining about 'all the Mexicans' and how they should all be shot . . ."

"You're kidding . . ."

"No, I'm not."

"What'd you say?"

"I said 'You wanna see a picture of my kids?' and I pulled out my wallet."

"You did not!" Laci gasped.

"Yes, I did."

"What'd he say?"

"He actually didn't have a whole lot to say after that."

She laughed.

"Tell Lily I love her," I said. I'd already talked to Dorito. "I wish I could say goodnight to her."

"I know," Laci sighed. We could video chat, but it wasn't the same.

I hung up thinking how hard it was not to be able to see Lily for so long and I was thinking about how much I hated not being able to talk to her on the phone. This wasn't the first time I'd gone to bed thinking these things, but that was the night I decided we really needed to do something about it.

~ ~ ~

WHEN I RETURNED home I was able to see for myself how great the combined youth group was. It was better than I'd hoped for. Not only did the kids seem excited about it, but they all worked together well. Just like Laci had said, the chemistry between them was just . . . different. By the time Easter was five weeks away even I could tell that the pageant was going to be great.

Meanwhile I was still playing racquetball with Tanner once or twice a week. One Wednesday night we were stuffing our gym bags into lockers when my phone went off. It was Laci.

Apparently Ashlyn had just called. She was supposed to watch Dorito for us starting the next afternoon because Laci and I were going to take Lily to a specialist in Minnesota to see if she was a good candidate for cochlear implants. Ashlyn wanted to let us know that Amelia was throwing up and had a fever of 103. She'd still be glad to watch Dorito, but . . .

No, thanks.

"Great," I complained, unzipping my racket cover. "Now one of us is going to have to stay with him in the waiting room every time she has a test or something and miss everything."

"Can't you take him in there with you?" Tanner wanted to know.

"Have you even *met* Dorito?" I asked. Not only did Dorito never shut up, but he immediately became friends with every person he ever came in contact with. It would be pretty much impossible for anyone to have a medical discussion, much less conduct any kind of hearing test on Lily, if Dorito was around.

"Why don't you have your parents watch him?"

"My mom and dad have to work and Laci's parents and Mrs. White are going to a church conference for three days."

"I could watch him," Tanner suggested.

"Yeah, right," I laughed.

"I'm serious."

"You hate kids!" I said, making the *Pon, Pon* signal at him.

"I don't *hate* kids," he argued, giving me the *Pon, Pon* signal right back. "I just don't want to have any of my own. They're fine as long as I know they're going to go away eventually."

"Are you serious? You'd really watch Dorito?"

"Sure."

"Don't you have to work on Friday?"

"I'll get a sub."

The next afternoon we pulled Dorito out of school after lunch and dropped him off at the high school with my mom. She was in the middle of her planning period, then Tanner had planning, then Charlotte would watch him after school until their faculty meeting was over and then . . .

"I guess they've got it all figured out," Laci sighed as we drove away.

"Too bad Dorito couldn't be a little more excited," I said and Laci laughed. He'd been so keyed up over staying with Tanner that he could hardly be bothered saying goodbye to us.

We drove along for a few minutes as Lily silently watched the cars passing.

"Listen to how quiet it is!" I said, and Laci laughed again.

Four hours later we arrived at Mike's apartment. We were going to spend the night with him so that we could get up bright and early the next morning for Lily's first appointment. As soon as Danica showed up we all went out to eat. The wedding was three weeks away and the girls talked endlessly over every detail.

"I wish you two would come visit more often," Danica said to both of us. Laci and Danica had only been around each other a few times, but they really liked each other a lot.

"Yeah," Mike teased. "The only time you ever come up is when you need something."

"You're one to talk," I said. "You've only been back to Cavendish *one time* since Laci and I moved back! You've even missed both of our lasagna bake-offs!"

"Tanner warned me about your lasagna," Mike said. "From what I hear I haven't really missed anything."

"Tanner's really glad you asked him to be your best man," I told Mike. "I can tell."

"I know," Mike nodded. "You were right."

"Of course I was right. I'm always right."

Mike rolled his eyes at me.

"So what's going on with him?" Mike asked. "Anything?"

"Nothing really," I shrugged. "I mean I see him all the time, but–"

"Yes," Laci interjected. "David's really been sacrificing to spend time with Tanner. He's had to go hunting and fishing and golfing and skeet shooting . . ."

"Don't forget racquetball," I reminded her.

"And he's been playing racquetball . . ."

Mike smiled at me. He knew I hadn't had a friend to do stuff with since Greg had died.

"He's actually watching Dorito right now if you can believe it," I said. "If *that* doesn't convince him he wants to settle down and have kids, nothing will!"

Everybody laughed.

Being doctors, Mike and Danica were both very interested in all of the appointments we had lined up at the Mayo clinic the next day. They had done a lot of research for us about cochlear implants and had asked around about the doctors who would be seeing Lily the

99

next day. Mike had even done rotations under one of the doctors and had nothing but good things to say about him.

Cochlear implants had been around for a long time, but they kept getting better and better every year. Through a surgical procedure, doctors could attach a series of tiny electrodes to the auditory nerve. These electrodes were attached to a receiver and then the incision site would be closed up. After a period of waiting for the site to heal, patients would get "activated". A magnet would attach a microphone, processor, and transmitter to the outside of the patient's head. The sound picked up by the microphone would pass from the processor to the transmitter, then to the receiver and then to the electrodes. The electrodes would stimulate the auditory nerve, and that would hopefully simulate hearing.

"If you decide to do it," Danica told Laci, "you should keep a blog about it."

"That would be me," I said, raising my hand. "Laci doesn't even know how to check her email."

"Oh, I do too."

No, she doesn't, I mouthed to Danica, shaking my head and Laci smacked my leg.

"Well," Danica laughed. "*You* should keep a blog about it then."

"No, thanks."

"Why not?" Mike asked.

"There's so much controversy about it . . . I really don't want to have to justify our decision to anybody. Whatever we decide – it's *our* business – not anybody else's."

So many people in the deaf community were completely against cochlear implants. Some felt that we should just accept Lily the way she was, that if we tried to "fix" her hearing we were implying something was "wrong" with her in the first place. Others believed that Scripture taught us to not alter our bodies in the way implants would do. Still others felt that we should wait until Lily was old

100

enough to make her own decision, but we knew that her language skills were developing *now* . . . .

Laci had even worried that other kids would tease Lily when they saw the external portion of her implants.

"Everybody'll just think she has a Bluetooth," I'd assured her and she'd laughed.

Laci had never been vain which is why I was a little surprised that she would worry over something so superficial. But I guess in reality we were both concerned about the challenges Lily was going to be facing in her life. She was a Latino being raised in a largely white community by white parents and she was deaf. I suppose Laci just didn't want Lily to have any additional hindrances.

When it came to her looks though, I really didn't think that Lily was going to have any problems. She was simply the most beautiful little girl to ever walk the face of the earth.

And I'm not just saying that because I'm her dad.

After all of the tests and procedures and exams, the doctors told us two things. The first was that Lily was profoundly deaf. We already knew that. This meant that for all intents and purposes she could hear nothing . . . even with hearing aids. The second thing we learned (and which we'd already suspected) was that she was an excellent candidate for implants.

"So have you decided anything?" Mike asked that evening. We were sleeping at his place again before driving home in the morning.

"First week in July," Laci nodded.

I glanced down at Lily who was sitting on the couch between me and Laci, looking at a catalogue of medical uniforms. I touched her cheek so that she turned to me and then I signed *I love you* to her and I mouthed it too. She smiled at me and went back to her catalogue.

I decided that – given the choice – Lily would want to be able to hear me say that.

When we got home I called Tanner.

"So you're still alive?" I asked him.

"Alive and well."

"Well, we're back. I'll come rescue you."

"Okay," he said. "We're at the high school."

"You're at the high school?"

"Hi Daddy!" I heard Dorito yell in the background.

"Yeah . . . down on the football field."

"Okay. See you in a little bit."

I figured he had some kind of practice going on and I was feeling bad that he'd had to take Dorito with him, but when I arrived it was only the two of them on the field. Tanner had a whistle around his neck and Dorito was wearing a miniature football uniform . . . complete with shoulder pads, helmet and cleats.

"Where did you get this?" I asked him, peering into his helmet to make sure he was really in there.

"Tan-man bought it for me!"

He spun around to show me the back. It said DORITO.

"Tan-man?"

"Uh-huh. That's what I call Tanner," he explained matter-of-factly. "It's a nickname."

I decided Tanner was right . . . our family had an issue with names.

"Watch this," Tan-man said, grinning at me. He blew his whistle and Dorito charged at a blocking sled with all his might. It moved forward three inches and then sprang back about ten. Dorito sprawled to the ground. He lay on his back like a turtle and grinned up at me through his helmet.

"Did you see that Daddy? I made it move!"

"Yeah," I laughed, grabbing his hands and helping him up. "It made you move too!"

"Oh, it always does that," Dorito said, and he crouched down into a starting position, ready to go again.

~ ~ ~

WHAT'S ALL THIS for?" Jordan asked me one evening. He had come over for one of our regular tutoring sessions and I was in the kitchen cutting cubes out of gelatin that were the same size as the sugar cubes I'd bought.

"Don't eat my science project!" I said, smacking his hand away.

"This is a science project?"

"Yep!" I grinned. "It's Career Week in kindergarten and I get to be a guest speaker tomorrow in Dorito's class."

"You're taking Jello and sugar cubes in to talk about being an engineer?"

"Uh-huh!" I smiled at him. He had a skeptical look on his face. "You're just dying to know how, aren't you?"

"If I listen can I have some Jello?" he asked.

I ignored him and started stacking gelatin cubes on top of one another making a little building on a metal tray.

"Here," I said, sliding the sugar cubes to him and tapping on the other half of the tray. "You make the same size building with these."

"Okay," I said when we were finished. "Now watch!"

I started shaking the tray back and forth until his little sugar cube building collapsed.

"What'd ya do that for?" he cried.

"I didn't do it. It was an earthquake."

He glanced at me sideways.

"See, we both made the same buildings, but they were made out of different materials so only one was able to survive."

"So you're going to teach them to make buildings out of Jello?"

"No, no, no. I'm trying to teach them that one of the important parts of my job is to make sure that the right materials are selected when it's being designed."

"Why don't you just have them use Lego's?" Jordan asked.

104

"You're missing the point."

"Are you going to build it or are the kids going to do it?"

"The kids are."

"And you really think they're not going to eat their buildings?"

"They can eat after the earthquake."

"And then you're going to go home and leave that poor teacher there with a bunch of sugared-up kids, aren't you?"

I smiled and nodded. He shook his head at me and I started cutting another row of cubes into the gelatin.

"You know," he said after a minute, glancing at his watch. "I think I should get going. You look kind of busy here . . ."

"No," I said. "I'm fine. I'm almost done."

"No, it's okay. I think I've pretty much got a handle on what we're doing right now and you need to get this finished, so I think I'm just going to get going."

"Are you sure?" I asked, stopping my cutting and looking up at him. "I've really got time . . ."

"No," he said again, heading into the living room. "You just keep working. I'll probably see you tomorrow."

Probably?

"Jordan's not coming over tonight either," I told Laci at dinner a couple of weeks later. This was about the fifth time he'd ditched me since I'd shown him my earthquake experiment.

"How come?"

"He claims he's rehearsing with someone."

"*Claims?*"

"He has like *two* lines, Laci. How much *rehearsing* does he need to do?"

Jordan had refused to be one of the Roman soldiers who had crucified Christ in our Easter pageant, so instead he was playing the thief on the cross who'd asked Jesus to remember him.

"Well, what do you think he's up to then?"

"I'm not sure," I admitted. "But I'm going to try and find out."

The weekend before Easter finally arrived and all of our regular babysitters were going to be at Mike and Danica's wedding. Fortunately Lydia was able to come over and stay with Dorito and Lily. I had a feeling she knew *exactly* what Jordan had been up to lately, but if she did, she wasn't letting on.

"Hi, Lydia!"

"Hi."

"Glad you could come babysit for us . . ."

"Anytime," she said.

"Usually Jordan helps us out a lot . . . it's been pretty convenient having him right across the street. He's really good with the kids . . ."

"Uh-huh."

Absolutely no reaction.

"Actually he hasn't been around quite as much lately. He seems pretty busy."

"Uh-huh."

"Of course he's got baseball and play practice . . ."

"Uh-huh."

"You pretty much ready for the play?"

"Yeah, I guess so."

"Been rehearsing outside of practice much?"

"Sort of."

"Any of the other kids?"

"I guess so."

Fine. Don't be helpful.

106

"You look very handsome in your tux," Laci told me later at the wedding reception. The band was playing a slow song and we were dancing.

"You don't look so bad yourself."

"Thanks."

I smiled at her.

"This is beautiful," she said, looking around the room.

I looked around too.

"Did you notice that the flowers on the cake match the ones in Danica's bouquet?"

"Uh-huh . . ."

"*You did?*"

"Uh-huh."

"Are you even listening to me?"

"Huh?"

"What are you looking at?" she asked. We stopped dancing and she followed my gaze across the room.

Jordan and Charlotte were *dancing* together.

"Oh, wow!" she said, turning back to me and smiling.

"Yeah," I said, still staring. "Wow!"

"Quit looking at them, David," she said, hitting me on the shoulder. We started dancing again.

"Oh, this is going to be fun!" I grinned.

"No, David. You are *not* going to tease them!"

"No," I agreed. "I'm not going to tease them . . . just *her.*"

"Oh, brother."

I waited until she was sitting next to her mom and when another slow song started I approached their table.

"May I have this dance, Charlotte?" I asked.

"Sure," she smiled.

"You're next," I promised, looking at Mrs. White.

"I'd better be."

Charlotte walked out onto the floor with me and we started dancing.

"So what was *that* all about?" I asked, grinning at her.

"Don't start with me, David or I'm not going to dance with you," she threatened.

"Oh, come on, Charlotte! Tell me . . ."

"What?" she sighed. "What do you want to know?"

"Everything!"

She rolled her eyes.

"There's hardly anything to tell!"

"*Hardly* anything?" I grinned.

"Yeah," she said, "hardly anything. We've been hanging out a bit and maybe we've kissed a couple of times."

"You've KISSED!?"

"Oh, brother," she said, rolling her eyes again.

"Well, well, well," I said, shaking my head. "So maybe Jordan's not the icky, disgusting boy you thought he was, huh?"

"Maybe," she admitted. "But please don't make a big deal out of this. *Please?*"

"Who? *Me?*"

"Yes . . . you!" She tried to glare at me, but wound up laughing instead.

"This explains a lot," I said. "Now I see why he's seemed so happy lately."

"Really?"

"Really. Any guy who's lucky enough to be with you is bound to be happy."

She smiled at me and we kept dancing until the song ended.

"You'd probably better go dance with my mom," she said.

"Yeah," I agreed, looking past her to where Jordan was standing, watching us. "I suppose I'd better."

The Monday after the wedding was a teacher workday and Tanner took the day off. He and Jordan and I had all decided to go fishing. Tanner pulled in across the street to pick us up and I headed over there while Jordan started putting his pole and tackle box into the bed of the truck. Their mom came out and gave Tanner, and then me, hugs.

"Why don't you boys come in and let me make you some breakfast?" she asked.

"Oh, no," Tanner said, shaking his head. "We can't do that, we've got to go to *Wilma's* . . . don't we Jordan?"

Jordan narrowed his eyes and glared at Tanner. I bit my lip and tried not to smile. Just because I wasn't going to tease Jordan didn't mean that I couldn't enjoy watching Tanner do it.

We pulled away and Tanner rolled down the windows and took a deep breath.

"Ahhh . . . do you smell that, Dave? It's springtime, and love is in the air."

I turned my head away and choked down a laugh.

"I hate you both," Jordan muttered.

"Whatdaya hate me for?" I cried, looking back at him. "I didn't say anything!"

"You were thinking it."

"I was thinking what?"

"Never mind. I don't know why I even agreed to go fishing with you two."

109

"Oh, I do!" Tanner said. "Because you knew we'd be going to *Wilma's* for breakfast!"

Tanner and I both laughed at him and he rolled his eyes, crossed his arms, and looked out the window for the rest of the way. I don't think he was really all that mad though and when we got to *Wilma's,* Jordan ordered a slushy and Charlotte brought him one.

~ ~ ~

MY BIRTHDAY WAS four days later . . . on Good Friday. I was more than a little disappointed to find out that Ashlyn had scheduled a full day of work for us at the church for scenery completion, dress rehearsal and a then a dinner for all the workers and kids that evening. I knew she'd picked Good Friday because everyone had the day off and lots of parents were going to be able to come by to help, but still . . .

"It's my *birthday*," I complained to Laci at breakfast before I left.

She smiled at me sympathetically.

"Maybe I'll leave early . . ."

"You can't just leave Ashlyn there in charge of everything all by herself!" Laci said. "Besides, it's not like we had anything special planned. I'll get someone to watch the kids tomorrow night and we'll go out and celebrate then."

"It won't be the same," I grumbled. "*Today's* my birthday."

Now I'd always liked Ashlyn – never had a problem with her – that is until my *birthday*. By the end of the day I was ready to smack her.

It was dark by the time we were finally finished with everything and she'd kept me hopping *all* day. At noontime I'd thought I might actually get away and eat lunch with my family, but she'd suddenly decided she needed me to set up the tables in the fellowship hall. Apparently it had to be done *right then* because the moms were going to be there any minute to set up for the dinner and she'd promised them the tables would be out when they arrived.

All day long she came up with one thing after another that she *really* needed me to do. Waves of people came and went, helping for a few hours and then leaving, while I stayed and worked and worked and worked . . . on my *birthday*.

Jordan and Charlotte managed to forget about each other long enough to wish me a happy birthday . . . barely.

At least I got to see Dorito (Jessica brought him and Cassidy by to practice with the children's choir) and my mom.

"Hi, honey. Happy birthday."

"Uh-huh," I said as she hugged me.

"What's the matter with you?"

"Nothing. Where's Dad?"

"Working."

"On Good Friday?"

"Yep."

He *was* an accountant and we *were* nearing the end of tax season, but that still didn't sound like Dad at all. I didn't get a chance to question her about it further though, because (*surprise, surprise*) Ashlyn needed me to do something.

When dinner time finally arrived I figured I could surely leave, but as I ran this idea past Ashlyn she confessed that the ladies had made me a birthday cake and they were going to be *very* disappointed if I left before dessert. After everyone sang *Happy Birthday* to me and I'd eaten my cake, Ashlyn all of a sudden remembered that she'd gotten her prints back from the wedding and I had to sit and look at them. *All* of them.

I was almost out the door when Ashlyn called my name from the other end of the fellowship hall.

What now?

I turned around. She had her phone up to her ear and was holding up one finger, signaling for me to hang on for a second.

I looked at my watch and sighed. The kids were probably already in bed.

"What?" I asked when she finally ended her call.

"I just wanted to wish you a happy birthday again," she smiled

112

"Thanks," I said, trying not to roll my eyes at her. I headed for the door before she could think up something else for me to do.

When I got home the house was quiet and I discovered that the kids were indeed in bed – already sound asleep. I went in and kissed Dorito on the forehead, picked up The Count off of the floor and tucked it back in bed with him. Then I went over to Lily's room and just stood there looking at her for a few moments. Feeling very sorry for myself, I realized that I hadn't even gotten to hold her all day.

I wandered into our bedroom, half expecting to find Laci sound asleep too, but she wasn't there. I went back into the empty living room and then into the kitchen. I even peeked down into the basement, but it was dark. Finally I called for her.

"Laci?"

"Out here," I heard her reply through the screen door that led from the kitchen to the back deck.

It was a cold spring night and I couldn't imagine *why* she'd left the sliding door partially opened or *why* she'd be out there all by herself. I went onto the deck and couldn't see her, but I heard something and turned to my left.

"Happy birthday," Laci said, smiling at me.

She was sitting in my new hot tub.

~ ~ ~

EVERYONE HAD BEEN told to bring their bathing suits when they came over the next afternoon for my birthday party. My dad, Laci's dad, my brother-in-law and Tanner all arrived about two hours early to finish the work they had not quite gotten done the day before. Apparently after the workmen had set up the hot tub and left, the four of them had spent the rest of the afternoon adding on to our existing deck so that it wrapped around and enclosed the hot tub.

They'd *almost* finished – they just had to complete the rails – but then Ashlyn had called.

Now I thought I'd been pretty civil to her all day, but either I'd been a lot shorter with her than I'd realized or she was very perceptive, because her exact words to Laci were: "If I try to keep him here any longer I think he's going to smack me."

Laci had told her to let me go home.

When they finished the rail they wood-burned their names and the date into the decking and my dad also burned Dorito's name into it because "he had helped a lot too".

Everyone showed up with a side dish and we grilled hot dogs and hamburgers. When Ashlyn saw me she asked if I was still angry at her.

"You're completely forgiven," I assured her.

"That's good," she said. "You shouldn't be mad at a pregnant woman."

"You're pregnant?"

She nodded and grinned.

"Congratulations!" After I gave her a hug she stepped into my new birthday present.

"You're not supposed to get in a hot tub when you're pregnant," I warned her.

"No, you're not supposed to let your body temperature get elevated," she corrected me. "I'm not going to stay in long enough to do that. I just want to try it out . . . I worked hard for this!"

"Two minutes," I said, looking at my watch. "Then I'm kicking you out."

"Deal," she said, sinking down into the water, leaning her head back and closing her eyes. "I'm going to enjoy my two minutes."

"He's got it bad, doesn't he?" Tanner asked, nodding toward Jordan. He and Charlotte had spent the entire afternoon together, soaking in the hot tub, walking around the yard or sitting on the grass. Right now they were each in a swing on the kids' play set, talking intently.

"Yeah," I agreed. "I think *she* does too."

"I don't think I've ever seen Jordan with so much to say in his entire life," Tanner laughed, shaking his head.

"I wonder what they're talking about?"

"Don't you read lips?" Tanner asked.

"No, that's Lily, remember?"

"Oh, yeah. You can only spy on people if they're talking in Spanish."

"I bet they aren't talking about how white their teeth are though," I grinned.

"No," Tanner said, laughing again. "Probably not."

"Look at 'em now," I said, nudging Tanner. Jordan was apparently trying to teach Charlotte how to sign. "Now if they start doing *that* I'll be able to tell you what they're talking about!"

"What's he saying?" Tanner asked.

"Um . . . I'm not sure . . ." I answered. Jordan kind of had his back to me.

"It's *Twinkle, Twinkle*," Dorito piped up from the other side of Tanner. He had a better view of the whole thing than I did.

"Are you sure?" Tanner asked him. "*Twinkle, Twinkle?*"

Jordan turned in his swing just enough so I could see what he was doing.

"Yep," I nodded. "He's right. It's *Twinkle, Twinkle.*"

"I cannot believe," Tanner said, shaking his head in disgust, "how *boring* it is to be a spy."

I had a nightmare in the middle of the night. I won't go into all of the gory details, but I dreamed that I couldn't find Lily and I realized I'd left the cover off of the hot tub and that she'd fallen in and drowned.

When I woke up my heart was pounding and even though I could hear her breathing over the baby monitor I had to get up to check on her anyway. Then I went into Dorito's room and checked on him too and then I went out onto the deck and made sure the cover was on the hot tub.

By the light coming from the kitchen I looked at the cover carefully and noticed for the first time that it had a place for a padlock, so I went into the garage and found one. I went back out to the hot tub, opened the lid and checked inside, closed it again and locked it with the padlock. Finally I sat down on the cover and lay back, listening to the hum of the filter and looking at the stars overhead.

"What are you doing out here?" I heard Laci ask me softly after a few minutes. I propped myself up on my elbows and smiled at her.

"I'm bonding with my hot tub."

She walked over and sat down next to me and then we both laid back and looked up at the sky.

"I put a lock on the cover," I said, holding the key over her face.

"Oh! That's a good idea. We can put it on the keychain with the freezer lock."

"Okay."

"So what were you thinking about out here?"

"Oh, I don't know."

"You think things are getting ready to fall apart, don't you?" she asked.

"What are you talking about?"

"You're worried something bad's going to happen."

"No, I'm not," I said, not too convincingly because I wasn't sure if she was right or not. "Why would you say that?"

"Remember how good things were right before Greg died?"

"What about it?" I asked.

"Well, this is the first time things have been really good for you since then," she said.

"No, it's not," I argued. "I've had lots of great things happen since then."

"I know," she agreed, "but there's always been something missing, like kids or friends or home . . ."

"Or you," I said, smiling at her.

"Exactly." She smiled back. "So now that you're finally happy again you're just waiting for something bad to happen."

"What are you now?" I asked her. "A psychiatrist?"

"Am I'm right?"

"Maybe a little," I admitted.

"So what's the worst thing that could happen?"

"Ummm . . . Lily could drown in my new hot tub?"

"You know what?" she asked, propping herself up on one elbow and looking at me. "Dorito and Lily and I could all get killed in a car accident tomorrow and I know you'd get through it and be all right."

"Okay, well then *that's* the worst thing that could happen . . . are you trying to be *comforting* here Laci? 'Cause I gotta tell ya, you're not doing a very good job . . ."

"We'd see each other again someday," she went on, quietly. "I just know that no matter what happens, everything's going to be okay."

She waited for me to nod and then she laid her head on my shoulder and I put my arm around her.

"Guess what?" she asked me after a moment.

"What?"

"It's Easter."

~ ~ ~

THE KIDS DID a fantastic job with the Easter pageant, and Tanner was at the service. I know he may have only been there to see Jordan perform, but it was still nice to see him in church for a change. We left from church and went directly to the airport for our visit to see Greg's grandmother.

Our flight left at three in the afternoon and it was dark by the time Greg's grandmother pulled into her driveway with us in her car. Dorito and Lily were both sound asleep, and Laci and I weren't too far from it ourselves. We tucked the kids into sleeping bags on the floor and crawled into the double bed in the guest room. In the morning we woke up with Dorito bouncing up and down between us.

"I wanna go to the beach! I wanna go to the beach!"

Greg's grandmother still had a lot of pictures on her mantle and Laci and I spent a few minutes looking at them before breakfast. There was a large one of Greg and Natalie at the prom, taken during our junior year in high school.

"Wow," Laci said, picking it up and holding it. "She looks so different now."

"That was ten years ago," I reminded her.

"I don't think *we've* changed that much, have we?"

We looked at each other for a moment and then shook our heads and laughed.

"I've got to get a picture of Charlotte and that new boy she's seeing," Greg's grandmother remarked, peering over Laci's shoulder.

"You mean Jordan?" I asked her.

"Yes, Jordan. Tell me all about this *Jordan*."

"He's the worst of sorts," I told her. "Nothing but trouble."

She raised her eyebrow at me.

"I'm just kidding. He's great."

"My Charlotte deserves the best."

"I know she does," I smiled. "He is."

After breakfast we took the kids to the beach. Lily was a little overwhelmed by the ocean and spent most of her time playing in the sand under Greg's grandmother's huge beach umbrella, but Dorito was absolutely beside himself.

"This is *SO COOL!*" he cried.

I grinned at him, "I know."

Laci thought it was pretty cool too . . . she'd never been to the beach before either.

We had someone take a picture of all five of us on the beach with my phone and then Laci took a video of me signing *"Ha, ha . . . you're not here!"* I sent them both to Charlotte, figuring she'd have Jordan translate for her.

The next day she sent me one back of her and Jordan and Hoover. Hoover's fur was purple . . . *completely purple!*

Jordan was signing back: *"Who's laughing now?"*

The next night Greg's grandmother took the kids out for pizza and insisted that Laci and I head to the beach by ourselves to watch the sunset. She packed us a picnic basket and sent us on our way.

We watched the sun drop over the Gulf of Mexico and then lay quietly for a few minutes.

"You know what I was thinking?" Laci asked after a while. I had my arm around her and my face was buried in her hair and neck.

"Hmmm?"

"How happy Greg would be if he could see us now."

I nodded.

"Do you think he knows?" she asked.

"I don't know. If he doesn't, he will one day."

"I hope he knows," she said. "I mean, we wouldn't even be together if it weren't for him."

"Yes, we would."

"You really think that?" she asked.

"I know that."

"How would we have gotten together?"

"I don't know, but we would have."

It was getting cold and we moved to one edge of our blanket, covering ourselves up with the rest because we weren't ready to go back yet.

Greg had spent five years pushing me and Laci together. I laughed whenever I thought of all the times Laci and I had just "happened" to wind up together. I could just about hear Greg now.

Hey Dad! When you make the plane reservations . . . put me and David and Laci next to each other . . . and put Dave in the middle!

Plus he'd quietly encouraged Laci for all those years . . . telling her that I'd come around one day and get over my stupid obsession with Samantha. Not to mention that he'd finally just come right out and told me what an idiot I was being for chasing after Sam instead of Laci.

I knew that God had wanted me and Laci to be together and I knew that He had used Greg to make that happen, but if He hadn't done it through Greg I still believed He would have done it some other way. I didn't know *how* it would have happened, but it would have happened.

Laying there with the stars and the waves and Laci – it was really . . . *perfect*.

I thought about how I couldn't have asked for anything more than I had with Laci and I thought about how thankful I was that God had decided I should be with her and I wondered again why He'd chosen to bless me so much.

But when Laci asked me what I was thinking about, I told her that I was just thinking about how much I loved her – which was true enough.

I didn't tell her everything else, but I hoped that she knew.

~ ~ ~

THE TUESDAY AFTER we got back from our spring vacation, Jordan and I were sitting at my work table when his phone rang. Hoover's fur had barely begun to fade, but I was still helping him with his math anyway.

"Hey . . . no, I'm over at Dave's . . . probably about another fifteen minutes, I'm just about done. Okay. Bye."

"Charlotte?" I asked, raising an eyebrow at him as he closed his phone.

"What's it to you?" he grinned.

"She's like a little sister to me, you know. I don't remember giving you permission to date her."

"Oh, you did," he assured me, still smiling. "You just don't remember because you're getting so old and you've got all that math stuff cluttering up your head."

"Uh-huh. So I gather she knows that I'm helping you with math?"

"Of course she does," he said, looking surprised that I'd ask. "Why wouldn't she?"

"I don't know," I shrugged. "I just wondered."

"Oh . . . I get it. You figured I wouldn't want her to know that I'm not a math genius like she is," he said, smiling again. "I think she pretty much had that figured out in the third grade."

"I just wondered," I said again, laughing and holding up my hands. "I wouldn't want to be the one to tell her something that you didn't want her to know about."

"Thanks," he said, smiling, "but don't worry about it."

He paused for a moment and then turned serious before finally saying, "I tell Charlotte *everything*."

The next time Jordan came over, Charlotte called him again. He promised her he'd be done soon and that he'd see her in a few minutes.

"Ya know, there's really no reason why *Charlotte* couldn't just help you with this stuff," I said, glancing at him, "since you two seem to have such a hard time being apart and everything . . ."

"We already tried that."

"And?"

"And it didn't go too good," he grinned.

"I use to help Laci with math all the time!"

"Really?" He looked at me quite skeptically.

"Uh-huh," I said, thinking back. "But I guess . . . well . . . maybe not so much after we actually started dating."

Jordan smiled again.

"You're right," I said, smiling back at him as I remembered. "That didn't go too good."

Charlotte came over one Friday night to babysit. Laci was upstairs with Lily when she got there and Dorito was bouncing up and down like a wild man.

"Is it okay if Jordan comes over?" she asked.

"Who?"

"Jordan."

"Jordan?" I asked, pointing my thumb toward the front door. "You mean Jordan from across the street?"

"Yes, David," she sighed.

"Why would you want Jordan to come over?"

She tilted her head at me and smirked.

"What?" I asked her.

"Can I stay up until you get home, Daddy?" Dorito begged.

124

"So is it okay if he comes over?" Charlotte asked.

"Can I, Daddy? Please? *Please?*"

I looked back and forth between them both. It was probably going to be after eleven by the time our movie ended and we got home. I doubted if Dorito would make it that long.

"You," I said finally, pointing at Charlotte, "can have Jordan come over, and you," I went on, pointing at Dorito, "can stay up and keep an eye on 'em."

Charlotte rolled her eyes at me and Dorito grinned.

When we got home that night the evening news was on TV and Jordan was sitting on the couch. Charlotte was sitting next to him, her head against his shoulder. Next to her, Dorito was slumped in her arms.

All three of them were sound asleep.

When school was over, Jordan came by with his final report card. He'd managed to pry himself away from Charlotte long enough to make a "B" on his geometry exam and finish out the semester with a low "A". I knew that if he didn't get any scholarship offers it wasn't going to be because of his math grades.

"Imagine how good you could've done if you hadn't skipped half of our tutoring sessions," I chided him, leaning down and picking up Lily who'd come to the door with me.

"I'm sorry," he said, looking dismayed.

"I'm just kidding, Jordan. You did great. Now go find Charlotte – enjoy your summer."

He smiled and started to leave.

"Hey," he said, turning around again. "When's Lily's surgery?"

"Two more weeks."

"So how long's she going to be in the hospital?"

"It's outpatient," I said, shifting her to my other side.

"Are you serious?"

"Yup," I nodded. "As long as everything goes okay."

"Oh," he said, nodding. "Everything's going to go okay."

He looked at Lily and smiled at her, signing as he spoke. *"I'm sure I learned all this sign language for nothing."*

~ ~ ~

A WEEK LATER the doorbell rang. I ignored it because Laci usually took care of everything like that while I was working. It rang again and Dorito poked his head into my office.

"Can I get the door?"

"Where's Mommy?"

"I don't know."

"I'll go with you," I said, standing up and following him as he raced into the living room. Laci emerged from the basement with a laundry basket full of clothes.

"Sorry," she said when she saw me.

"Charlotte!" Dorito cried as he opened the door.

"Hi, Dorito," Charlotte said, glancing into the room and spotting me. She stepped into the living room and looked at Laci. "Hi."

"Hi, Charlotte," Laci said.

"What's up?" I asked.

"Ummm," her voice caught and I could tell something was wrong. She looked down at Dorito. He was jumping up and down, trying to get her to pick him up.

"Hey, Dorito," I said. "Go in your room and play with your train."

"I wanna play with Charlotte," he said.

"*Now*, Dorito!"

The sharpness in my voice startled him and he went to his room. Charlotte was looking down, as if he were still there at her feet.

"What's wrong, Charlotte?"

She completely lost it. She drew her hands up to her face and just started sobbing. Laci dropped the laundry basket and we both led her over to the couch.

"What's wrong?" I asked her again. I figured she'd had a fight with Jordan or something.

"I'm pregnant," she sobbed.

Did NOT see that coming.

"I don't know what to do," she cried. "I don't know what to do!"

"Does your mom know?" Laci asked softly.

Charlotte shook her head no.

"You have to tell her," Laci said and Charlotte shook her head some more.

"Does Jordan know?" I asked.

Charlotte shook her head again.

"He needs to know too," I said.

"No," she said, starting to cry harder.

"Yes, Charlotte," I said. "This is his responsibility too . . . he needs to know."

"No," she wept. "It's not his . . ."

Now my head was spinning.

"How far along are you?" Laci asked her quietly.

"I don't know. Maybe three or four months?"

She couldn't be that far along . . . *could she?* She wasn't even showing . . .

"Have you been to see a doctor yet?" I asked.

"No . . ."

"You've got to go see a doctor."

"I don't have any money," she cried.

"Charlotte," Laci said, "I'm sure your mom's got insurance on you . . ."

"NO!" she wailed. "I can't tell my mom. My mom can NOT find out about this!"

I think she'd been deluding herself into actually thinking that maybe she could just disappear for a few months and then come home without her mom ever finding out what had happened – we

128

were probably fortunate that she hadn't run away or something. It took a while, but we finally convinced her that there was no way her mom was not going to find out.

She agreed to let me go get Mrs. White while Laci waited with her at our house. It was four blocks to Greg's (I would always think of it as Greg's). Four *long* blocks.

"Hi, David," Mrs. White said, smiling brightly at me as she opened the door. "Come in!"

"Actually," I said, "would you mind coming over to our house?"

"Is everything okay?"

"Ummm, let's talk about it at my house."

"Are the kids okay?

"They're fine . . ."

"It's not Laci, is it?" she asked worriedly.

"Laci's fine."

"Please tell me her cancer's not back . . ."

"No," I said, smiling slightly. "It's nothing like that."

"Well, what's wrong then?"

"Can we please just go to my house?" I asked. "Please?"

She finally nodded and closed the door behind her.

"You're making me nervous," she said as we set off down the sidewalk.

"Don't be nervous."

"Why won't you tell me what's wrong?"

"I'm sorry," I said. "Everything's going to be fine."

It was an even *longer* four blocks home. When we finally got to our house we stepped into the living room where Dorito and Lily sat mesmerized in front of the television, watching some show Laci usually avoided letting them see.

"Laci?

"In here," she called from my office.

I led Mrs. White down the hall and stepped through the door. Charlotte was sitting on the couch in my office and she started sobbing again as soon as she saw her mother, burying her face back into her hands. I let Mrs. White step past me and then I went back out into the hall and closed the door after me because I really didn't want to be there.

Laci came out almost right behind me and together we walked down the hall to watch television with our kids.

~ ~ ~

AT YOUTH GROUP on Sunday night Ashlyn called everyone together and settled them down. It had been apparent from the bits and pieces of conversation that we'd heard that everyone already knew, so she just went right ahead and addressed it. Ashlyn told them that Charlotte needed their prayers and support right now and that we'd better not hear anyone saying something behind Charlotte's back that they wouldn't say to her face. I looked around at their faces and most of them were nodding. Lydia was crying.

After she'd finished talking to them about Charlotte, Ashlyn got the evening's program underway. She passed out copies of the finalized calendar for the summer and before she started going over it with them she handed the extras to me. I folded one of them up and put it in my pocket, deciding I'd take it over to Jordan's house when we were done.

It was the first youth group meeting that I ever remembered him missing.

I knocked on the door and Jordan's mom answered.

"Hi, David," she said, smiling at me.

"Hi."

"Come on in . . ."

"Thanks . . . I just wanted to give Jordan a copy of our calendar. We missed him at youth group tonight."

"Oh!" she said. "That's nice of you. He decided to stay home, I don't think he's been feeling too good the last couple of days. I'm not sure exactly what's wrong with him."

I'll bet I know . . .

"Is he home?"

"He's up in his room," she said, nodding toward the stairs. "You can go up if you want . . . I don't think he's contagious or anything."

Probably not.

I trudged up the steps and knocked on his door.

"Yeah . . ."

I opened the door and peered into his room. He was lying on his bed, holding a baseball. He looked at me.

"Can I come in?"

He nodded, sat up, and stared at the wall. He was still clutching the baseball in one hand.

I tossed the youth group schedule onto his desk, turned his desk chair around and sat down in it, leaning forward with my elbows on my knees. I didn't say anything.

"She knew . . ." he finally said, glancing at me.

"What do you mean?"

"I mean she *knew* . . . she knew the whole time. She knew before Easter . . . she knew before the wedding . . . she knew before we even started going out. She knew the *whole time!*"

"Are you sure?" I asked, finding that pretty hard to believe.

"Yes, I'm sure! She told me! I asked her how long she'd known and she told me!"

"So you've talked to her . . ."

"Yeah," he said, giving me a short, disgusted laugh and lying back down on the bed. "I've talked to her."

He tossed the baseball into the air above his head and caught it.

I really didn't know what to say so I kept quiet. He kept tossing the baseball.

"You know," he said after a moment. "What bothers me the most is that she didn't tell me. I mean, yeah . . . I probably would've been upset to find out that she'd slept with him or that she was pregnant or whatever. But I think I could have gotten over that . . . you know?"

He glanced at me just quick enough to see me nod.

"What gets me," he said, still throwing the ball, "is that she let me . . ."

He stopped talking and stopped tossing the ball.

"She let you what?"

He stared at the ball for a long time.

"She let me get close to her." he said very quietly, not taking his eyes off the ball. "She *knew* she was going to hurt me and she just let me get close to her anyway."

"I'm sorry, Jordan."

He started tossing the ball again.

"I was so stupid," he said, shaking his head. "I was just *so* stupid."

"You weren't stupid, Jordan."

"Yes, I was! You know what I did?"

I shook my head at him.

"I told her *all* about the conference you took me to and I told her what I'd decided and do you know what she said?"

I shook my head again.

"She thought it was a *great* idea! As a matter of fact, everything I ever told her . . . everything I ever shared with her . . . she was right on board with whatever I said. I couldn't believe how much we had in common and I was thinking to myself 'Wow! This is unbelievable.' I mean I've known her my whole life, but all of a sudden it was like God was showing me how *perfect* she was for me."

He sat up on the edge of the bed and paused for a moment.

"I actually thought I loved her," he finally said, shaking his head again. "Now *that* was stupid."

133

"It wasn't stupid . . ."

"You know what?" he asked, ignoring me. "The worst part is that she pretended that she loved me too . . ."

"I don't think she was pretending, Jordan . . ."

"You don't do that to someone that you love! You just *don't!* How could you do something like that to somebody that you love?"

"Look, Jordan, I don't have all the answers," I said, shaking my head. "There's nothing I can say that's going to make everything all better. I just . . . I just came over here tonight because I wanted to let you know that I'm here if you need anything."

He stood up and turned his back to me so that I couldn't see his face.

"Thanks," he said, walking over to his desk. He picked up the schedule I'd thrown there earlier and started unfolding it. "What's this?"

"Our calendar for the summer."

"Thanks," he said again, "but I don't think I'm going to be going to youth group anymore."

He crumpled it up and threw it toward the hoop on his wall. It swished through the net and landed in the trashcan underneath.

~ ~ ~

BY THE NEXT day I was as close to being angry with Charlotte as I'd ever been in my life and before I rang the bell I prayed for God to please not let me yell at her.

Mrs. White answered the door.

"Any chance you're here to talk to Charlotte?" she asked and I nodded.

"That's good," she said. "She thinks you hate her."

"Why in the world does she think I hate her?"

"She thinks everybody hates her," Mrs. White explained, smiling slightly and I softened immediately.

"Where is she?"

"Down in the basement . . . ironing. She's trying to make herself as miserable as possible."

"Punishing herself?"

"Exactly."

"Can I go down there?" I asked, pointing toward the basement door.

"I wish you would."

She must not have heard the doorbell. I trudged down the stairs, but she apparently figured it was just her mom because she didn't look up from her ironing. When I looked carefully, I could tell – just barely – that she was pregnant.

I spoke her name and when she realized I was there she let go of the iron and started crying.

I walked over to her and set the iron upright, unplugged it and then wrapped my arms around her.

"It's okay, Charlotte."

"No, it's not," she sobbed into my shoulder.

"Come over here and sit down." We walked over to the steps and I kept one arm around her.

"I was going to go to college and be an engineer," she said, covering her eyes. "I was going to make my dad and Greg so proud."

I'd always had a feeling that was what was going on, but I'd never really been sure.

"Did you know that I'm number three in my class?" she went on. "I was going to take AP Physics and AP Calculus this fall . . . those are *weighted* classes. If I did good enough in them I could have been valedictorian."

"You're just pregnant, Charlotte . . . you're not dying. There's no reason you can't still do all that."

"I'm not going back to school," she said, shaking her head.

"You don't have to," I told her. "My mom says the school has to provide you with a homebound teacher if you ask for one . . . and she said she'd be glad to help you and you know I will . . ."

That made her cry harder for a moment, but I think it also made her feel better because soon she started calming down.

"Have you been to see a doctor yet?"

She nodded.

"When are you due?"

"December . . ."

The same month Ashlyn was due. I could hardly believe she was that far along already. It seemed that Ashlyn was showing a lot more, but I guess Ashlyn hadn't been trying to hide it.

"Why didn't you tell anyone?" I asked her, coming around to the real reason for my visit.

She started to cry again.

"Why didn't you tell Jordan?"

"When?" she asked, angrily. "At what point in our relationship was I supposed to bring *that* up?"

"I . . . I don't know, Charlotte, but how could you start something up with him and not tell him?"

"I didn't '*start something up with him*'!" she cried. "It just . . . it just *happened!*"

136

"But you really knew? The whole time?"

"I guess so," she admitted, wiping her eyes. "I kept trying to convince myself it wasn't true, but I knew . . .

"Jordan hates me," she finally mumbled.

"Nobody hates you, Charlotte. We all hate that you're going through this, and we hate to see you hurting, but nobody hates *you*."

"Jordan does."

"It's different for Jordan," I admitted. "Laci and I are hurting for you and you're mom's hurting for you. Jordan's hurting for you too, but he's also hurting for himself. He doesn't hate you though."

"Did he say that?"

"He didn't have to," I said. "I can tell."

~ ~ ~

TANNER AND I went fishing the next week. I'd invited
Jordan, but he was pretty much refusing to do anything besides pout,
so it was just the two of us. We went to Makasoi Lake. I couldn't
figure out why Tanner never wanted to go to Cross Lake, but since
we always used *his* boat which was on *his* trailer pulled by *his* truck, I
couldn't really argue much. He hardly talked for the entire trip up
there. I figured he was just sore because three days earlier I'd finally
beaten him at racquetball.

We'd been out on the water for about ten minutes when Tanner
cut the engine. He went to the front of the boat and dropped the
trolling motor down; then he guided us into a cove and threw his line
past a submerged log.

I was still rigging a plastic worm on my line when he spoke.

"Megan's pregnant."

There was a loud "clunk" as my bullet sinker hit the bottom of
the boat.

"You're kidding . . ."

"Nope." He shook his head.

I wasn't sure what to say. I had a feeling congratulations weren't
in order and I decided that *"How did this happen?"* wasn't going to
sound too intelligent either.

Ashlyn . . . Charlotte . . . Megan . . .

Man . . . what was going on?

"Wow . . ." I finally managed to say.

"Yeah," he said. "Tell me about it."

"What are you going to do?"

"We haven't decided yet."

"You're . . . you're not thinking about . . ."

"No," he said, shaking his head at me. "That's not on the table."

138

I probably should have known that if they were thinking about having an abortion he never would have even let me know that she was pregnant. I don't know why it wasn't "on the table", but I was glad it wasn't.

"So are you going to get married?"

"No," he said. "I already told you that I don't want to do the family thing."

A little too late for that . . .

If I'd felt like being mean I could have given him the *Pon, Pon* signal, and as it was I almost told him that it looked like the "family thing" was happening whether he wanted it to or not.

Be supportive . . . be a good friend.

"I'm sorry," I said. "I know this isn't what you wanted to have happen."

His lure reached the boat and he threw it out again.

"You can say that again."

~ ~ ~

NO LONGER ANGRY at Charlotte I started getting mad at Jordan instead. I knew he was hurt and I knew he had every right to be, but at some point he was just going to have to suck it up and deal with it.

Usually when I was working in my office I could hear the clanking of his weight set or the constant *thwap* of baseballs hitting the tarp in his back yard. Now there was nothing but silence and I never saw Jordan leave the house.

Tanner even said that when a recruiter from the University of Minnesota came to talk with the family Jordan barely had two words to say. Tanner also told me that Jordan had *turned down* an interview with the recruiter from State.

Everybody knew that Charlotte was planning on going to State, but still . . .

The following Friday, Ashlyn, Brent, Laci and I took the combined youth group to Six Flags. Charlotte didn't go, but neither did Jordan. True to his word, he hadn't gone to a single youth group meeting all summer.

When we walked past the pitching booth I stopped and watched. There were five or six high school boys there, each taking turns throwing the ball at a target and giving each other high fives whenever they threw one over seventy-five. Ashlyn, Brent and Laci asked me if I wanted some ice cream, but I didn't so they left me there for a few minutes while they walked to a nearby vendor.

No one was even close to being as good as Jordan. I watched them throw ball after ball and I got madder and madder at him.

When they came back with their ice cream they asked me if I was ready to go.

I was ready to do *something* . . . I just didn't know what it was yet.

The next day I opened Laci's jewelry box and rifled around in it for a minute. It didn't take me long to find what I was looking for . . . a crude star necklace made from a paperclip and string. A little girl who lived in the landfill in Mexico had given it to Laci when Greg's dad had taken our youth group down there. Ashlyn and Natalie and Mike and Laci and Greg and I had all gone . . . we'd only been fourteen years old.

"I called Aaron," I told Laci when she found me lying on the bed holding the star necklace. Aaron was the coordinator of the Christian outreach program in Mexico. He'd been our group leader when we'd gone and Laci's boss years later when she'd worked for them.

"You did?"

I nodded.

"Why?"

"I think our youth group needs to go down there."

"Really?" she asked, sitting down on the edge of the bed.

I nodded again.

"When?"

"They've got a slot open right before Christmas . . ."

"We'd be gone over Christmas? That's right when Ashlyn's due."

And Charlotte . . .

I nodded one more time.

"I don't think we've got enough time to raise all the money we'd need." she said.

"Most of these families could pay for whatever we don't raise."

"What about the rest?"

I just looked at her.

"Gonna sell your hot tub?" she asked, smiling.

"I don't think it'll come to that."

"Are you sure you want to be away from home over Christmas?"

"I really think we need to do this . . ."

"Are we taking the kids?"

"I thought maybe we'd take Dorito and leave Lily here with your mom. I think he'd really like to go see everybody at the orphanage again."

"We wouldn't be with Lily on Christmas Day?"

I said it one more time.

"I really think we need to do this."

The next day I walked over Jordan's house. He was out in the driveway, changing the oil in his mom's car.

"I want you to come to youth group tonight."

"No," he said, not looking up from under the hood. "I don't think so."

"Well, I *do* think so. You need to be there tonight. I'll pick you up at five-thirty."

He didn't say anything.

"Don't worry," I went on. "Charlotte's not going to be there."

"Why not?" he asked, finally looking at me. I could tell that for the briefest moment he was worried something had happened to her.

"Because . . . it's an organizational meeting for a mission trip we're taking and she's not going to be able to go."

"Where are we going?"

"Mexico."

"We are?"

"Yeah."

He thought about it for a moment and then nodded.

"Okay."

I nodded back at him. "See you at five-thirty."

~ ~ ~

LILY'S SURGERY WAS three days later. We went up the night before and stayed with Mike and Danica in their new house. I wasn't nervous about her surgery at all ... I just knew somehow that everything was going to be alright.

I was more worried instead, about Ashlyn's baby. Ashlyn and Charlotte had both had AFP tests done. The test had checked for abnormal levels of proteins that could indicate a problem. Charlotte's tests had come back fine, but Ashlyn's . . .

"It showed there's a chance her baby's going to have Down's syndrome," Laci had told me.

"A chance?"

"A ten percent chance."

"What are they going to do?"

"Nothing. They could have an amniocentesis if they wanted to find out for sure ahead of time, but there's like a one or two percent chance that could make her lose the baby, and since they're going to have him no matter what, they're just going to wait."

"That's going to be a long, hard wait," I said.

"It is," Laci agreed.

Lily's surgery went off without a hitch – just like I knew it would. The doctors shaved off a bit of hair behind her ears (which freaked Laci out just a little bit) and made an incision. Then they attached electrodes to her auditory nerves and implanted a little receiver and a magnet the size of a pea. After she was stitched up they brought her out from under the anesthesia and they took us back to see her. She didn't seem to be in any pain at all, but she kept signing to us over and over that she was thirsty.

144

Two nights later we took the kids to the city park to watch fireworks. Lily's incision had to heal for about three weeks and then would come her "activation day". That would be the day that she would get the external parts to her implants (the tiny microphones and transmitters) and the day we would begin the long process of helping her to hear as a well as possible.

Right now though, she sat on my lap, watching the lights burst in the sky. I knew she could feel the explosions, but I hoped that by this time next year she would be hearing them loud and clear.

~ ~ ~

THREE WEEKS AFTER Tanner told me that Megan was pregnant we went fishing again. Jordan didn't go with us this time either . . . he was still feeling too sorry for himself to go out and enjoy anything. That was fine. I figured that if nothing else, a trip to the landfill in Mexico around Christmas time was going to fix that.

Tanner picked me up at my house and this time he didn't wait until we were on the lake to tell me what he had to say.

"Megan moved out," he said after we'd barely pulled out of the driveway.

"*Why?*"

"We're through," he shrugged.

"What about the baby?"

"She says she lost it."

"She *says* she lost it?"

"I don't think she was ever pregnant," he said. "I think she was lying about it so I'd marry her and when that didn't work she conveniently 'lost it.'"

"Are you serious?"

"Yeah," he said. "I'm pretty sure."

"Well, what would she have done if you *had* married her?"

"I think she would have 'lost it' after we got married."

"I don't know what to say."

"You don't have to say anything."

We rode along quietly for a few minutes.

"Jordan says you guys are going to Mexico over Christmas?" he finally asked, breaking the silence.

"Yeah."

"You need another chaperone?"

"Why?" I asked, trying not to act shocked. "You wanna go?"

"I was thinking about it."

146

The last thing I wanted to do was to discourage him from going, but . . .

"You know, Tanner," I said, "I'm not sure if you realize what things are like down there . . ."

"I know what it's like."

Of course he knew . . . it wasn't as if he'd never heard any of us talk about it before.

"Well, yeah," I said, nodding. "We could use another chaperone. That'd be great."

"Great," he said.

"Great," I said again.

Everything was just great.

~ ~ ~

ACTIVATION DAY CAME – the day they would hook Lily up to her transmitters and see if the surgery had been a success. We knew it was just the beginning of what was going to be a long process in helping her to hear, but it was pretty exciting just the same.

First the technologist attached little magnets to either side of Lily's head, right over the implants. These held the microphones and transmitters in place. She also hooked her up to some equipment that would allow her to determine if Lily was sensing anything, even if she didn't visibly react.

At first Lily was just introduced to computer generated sounds that we couldn't even hear, but I could tell every time one was made because of the look on her face.

"Okay," the technologist said. "She's definitely sensing those. Let's see how she does with some ambient sounds now."

Ambient sounds were normal sounds . . . ones not generated by the computer.

"Which one of you wants to talk to her first?" she asked, looking at us.

Laci and I looked at each other.

"You go ahead," I told Laci and she smiled.

Lily was playing with the technologist's I.D. card that was clipped onto the pocket of her shirt. The technologist made an adjustment to each transmitter and then nodded at Laci. Laci glanced at me first and then spoke softly.

"Lily? Hey, Lily . . . can you hear me?"

Lily let go of the I.D. card and it was a wonderful moment.

She looked *right at* Laci.

We left Mike and Danica's the next morning and after we'd been home for an hour or so, Jordan knocked on the door . . . *very quietly*.

"I wanted to know how things went," he whispered. He was holding a stuffed animal with a red bow around its neck

I laughed at him, glad to see that he'd finally gotten out of the house.

"You don't have to whisper."

"But I thought it might all be too much for her . . ."

"She's doing good. Come on in."

Lily had heard us at the door and she'd turned around. When she saw that it was Jordan she smiled at him.

"Hi, Lily," he said, signing it too. "Oh, I guess I don't need to sign it anymore."

"No, you should, actually," Laci said. "That's how she's going to learn what we're saying – by reading lips and having us sign while we talk to her."

"Okay," Jordan smiled. "So it went good? She can hear now?"

"Well," Laci explained, "she's definitely responding. She's got to go through a series of mappings to figure out what the best settings are going to be . . ."

"Mappings?"

"It's really complicated," I told him. "I've been studying up on it for two months and I still don't understand it."

"But she's definitely hearing stuff," Laci went on. "And nothing's seemed to bother her yet either, which we were really worried about . . ."

He sat down on the floor next to Lily, handed her the stuffed animal, and started talking and signing to her. He still talked very quietly.

"Here," I said after a little while. "Watch."

I sat behind her with a toy drum that belonged to Dorito. I hit it with the wooden mallet and Lily swiveled her head around to see where the noise had come from.

I moved to the couch and Jordan continued sitting on the floor with her for another minute or two until the doorbell rang. Lily looked up again when it did and Laci answered the door. Jordan also turned around to see who it was.

It was Mrs. White and Charlotte.

Jordan turned back around to face Lily. Out of habit to get her attention he stroked her cheek before he spoke to her.

"Good bye, Lily," he said, and he signed it. Then he got up and went into the kitchen and never looked back. I heard the sliding glass door open and then close behind him.

When I turned back to face Charlotte and Mrs. White, Charlotte met my eyes.

"Gee, Dave. I guess you were right," she said. "He doesn't hate me at all."

~ ~ ~

SCHOOL BEGAN IN the fall and Jordan and Charlotte both started their senior year of high school. Mrs. White had said that under no circumstance was Charlotte going to have a homebound teacher. She said the taxpayers weren't going to pay big bucks just because Charlotte wanted to be spared some embarrassment. I knew Charlotte wasn't the first girl to ever walk the halls of Cavendish High School pregnant (she wasn't even in the first one hundred), but I also knew that it was hard for her.

Charlotte's old boyfriend – the father of the baby – was named Garret (or maybe Jarret – I was never actually too clear on that). Apparently he and his parents sat down with Charlotte and Mrs. White and they all decided that the baby should be put up for adoption – a closed adoption. After the baby was born and Charlotte left the hospital, she would never see her baby again.

And after that, Charlotte changed.

She quit her job at *Wilma's*. She quit laughing. She quit joking around. She became reserved – a word that never would have been used to describe her before. For her entire life, Charlotte had always been brimming with confidence, but now she hardly talked with anyone except for those who were closest to her.

At some point along the way, however, she also quit punishing herself and resolved that nothing was going to keep her from making her dad and Greg proud. With no social life and no job, she was able to devote herself to her school work and she studied her heart out.

151

That happened to make me proud too.

Meanwhile, Jordan's attitude finally improved. He showed no signs of ever forgiving Charlotte, but he seemed to have decided that he wasn't going to mope around anymore either. He had two more math classes to take this year. The first one was technical math (i.e. easy math) – and he knocked on the door after the first day of school with a big smile on his face.

"You're gonna *love* this!" he said.

"Love what?"

"My math project."

"You have a math project?" I could barely keep the excitement out of my voice.

"Yep!"

"What is it?"

I couldn't believe how lax the requirements were (it's no wonder we lag behind the rest of the world when it came to math). All he had to do was build something using blueprints he'd made himself. *Big deal.*

Of course I was going to turn it into a big deal and Jordan knew that. We were going to make something *great.*

"Got any ideas?" I asked him.

"Well," he said. "It's due right before Christmas, so I was thinking about building something that we could take to the orphanage and donate to them after I got a grade, but if I made a dollhouse or something like that it would be too big to get down there."

"Yeah," I agreed. "You're probably right . . . plus, the kids really don't need any more *stuff* . . ."

"Do they need money?" Jordan asked. "Maybe I could make something and sell it here or auction it off and then give them the money."

"Well, of course they always need money, but what they really need are . . ."

"What?"

I sighed. "Parents."

"I'm afraid I can't help them there," Jordan said, sighing too.

We sat quietly for a minute and I thought about one set of parents who had come to the orphanage from Delaware. Like almost every mom and dad who came to pick up a child, they'd been beside themselves with excitement. They were adopting a little girl, who happened to be a good friend of Dorito's.

Now I normally didn't make small talk with people I was never going to see again (what's the point?), but Dorito had been pretty upset that this particular little girl was leaving and I'd wound up talking with the parents while Dorito gabbed with her and hugged on her for a few more minutes. During that time I'd learned that the only reason they'd even been able to adopt was because of an organization called Shaohannah's Hope.

Shaohannah's Hope was named after the first little girl adopted by Steven Curtis Chapman and his wife. It was a non-profit, designed to help Christian families adopt (despite how expensive it was). They'd told me all about how the organization had provided a grant to offset some of the costs and how they never would have been able to adopt without Shaohannah's Hope. I remembered thinking at the time that if more people could get help like that then maybe our orphanage wouldn't be quite so full.

"You know what, Jordan?" I finally asked. "I think maybe you *can* help them there."

He loved the idea of building something, selling it, and donating the proceeds to Shaohannah's Hope. The next question was: What to build?

We nixed the whole dollhouse idea early on (too girly). Then we talked about building a gazebo, but didn't think anyone was going to buy one of those in the dead of winter. Finally he decided to make a series of buildings that could go with an electric train set. We went to the hobby shop and determined that something in an "O" scale would probably sell best at Christmas time. The hobby shop owner even offered to help him sell it, so Jordan and I got to work.

When Laci learned what we were doing, she said she'd see me in December.

It *was* a busy fall. Lily had intensive therapy with her cochlear implants, Dorito started first grade, and Laci was so excited about our mission trip that she managed to attend every youth group meeting we had even though Ashlyn wasn't there. Laci and I were meeting each week with the kids from the combined youth group who *were* going to Mexico, while Ashlyn and Brent held regular meetings at their church with the kids who *weren't* going. Ashlyn and Brent's group was working on a Christmas play, while our job was to come up with a program and activities to do with the kids at the orphanage and the kids at the landfill.

Assured that he wouldn't be running into Charlotte, Jordan attended every meeting too. When we started discussing program ideas, Jordan spoke up and said he really wanted to do something involving sign language. Everybody in the group got quiet while I called Inez (the director of the orphanage), and asked her if there were any deaf children in the orphanage right then.

"No, Señor David, but by Christmas time . . . who knows? We do have a little blind girl right now . . ."

154

I had this sudden image of Laci convincing me that I needed to learn Braille.

"Thanks, Inez. I was just wondering."

"We can't wait to see you!!" she said before I hung up.

"No deaf kids right now," I told everyone, and Jordan looked crestfallen.

"There's no reason we still can't do something with sign language," Laci said. "We'll teach the kids things to use when they do meet someone who's deaf . . ."

"Like what?" someone wanted to know.

"We could do some Christmas carols," Jordan suggested.

"Yeah," Lydia said. "We'll look just like the Happy Hands Club on *Napoleon Dynamite*."

Everyone laughed and Jordan seemed almost happy.

The kids got pretty fired up about signing. The EC teacher who had taught Jordan agreed to come to our youth group meetings once a week and work with the kids. They learned five different Christmas carols *and* the Christmas story. One of the guys happened to play the guitar and two of the girls played in the marching band (one the flute and one the clarinet.) All three started bringing their instruments and by the time Thanksgiving rolled around we were sounding (and looking) pretty good. They even made a set of flashcards showing a bunch of the signs we'd be teaching the kids. We glued them onto construction paper and had them laminated so we could leave them with the kids at the orphanage before we left.

Two weeks before we were to leave Jordan turned in eight little "O" scale buildings: a church, a depot, a warehouse, a school, and four houses. After his teacher gave him his "A" he turned them over to the hobby shop owner who put them on display in the front window of his shop with a sign explaining where all the proceeds from their sale would go. Three days later he called Jordan and told him that not only had someone bought all eight pieces, but that several people had made donations for Shaohannah's Hope. Jordan mailed a check off a week before we left.

The morning we were to leave, Laci's phone rang while she was in the shower. I looked at it, saw that it was Ashlyn, and answered it.

"They're on their way to the hospital," I told Laci when she got out.

"They who?"

"Ashlyn and Brent ."

"Oh."

"Ashlyn's gonna have a baby!" Dorito shouted as soon as Jordan climbed into the car. Laci was sitting in the back seat with him.

"Like *now*?" Jordan asked, looking back at Laci.

"Apparently," she nodded.

"Oh . . ."

"She's gonna keep her baby," Dorito said. I don't think I'd ever seen him so excited . . . he was really wound up. "Charlotte's gonna have a baby too, but she's not gonna keep hers."

Jordan did up his seatbelt and I pulled out of the driveway.

"Charlotte's baby's going to be adopted," Dorito went on. "I was adopted. I used to live in an orphanage."

"I know," Jordan said, looking out the window.

156

"Charlotte's baby's just gonna get adopted. It's not gonna live in an orphanage."

"I know."

"We're gonna go see where I use to live."

"I know."

"There's lots of kids there," he explained. "You can adopt one if you want to."

"I think I'll probably wait until I'm married before I do that," Jordan said, looking back at him and smiling slightly.

"You could marry Charlotte," Dorito suggested. "Then you could adopt *her* baby."

Jordan turned around and looked out the window again.

"You know what, Dorito?" I asked him.

"What?"

"You talk a lot."

"I know," he said, matter-of-factly.

"Maybe you could be quiet until we get to the airport."

"Okay," he sighed.

"Don't worry," I assured Jordan. "He's sitting next to me and Tanner on the plane."

"Does *Tanner* know that?" Jordan asked.

"I thought I'd surprise him."

"You're not serious, are you?"

"No," I laughed, shaking my head. "He knows. Dorito begged him."

On the plane ride Tanner taught Dorito how to play crazy eights. They also played tic-tac-toe, thumb wrestled, and played with Tanner's phone, taking pictures and videos and trying all the games. When Dorito *finally* fell asleep it was with his head resting against Tanner, even though I was sitting right on his other side.

It had been five months since Megan had "lost" the baby and moved out. I decided that was long enough. When Tanner put his arm around Dorito's little body I smiled at him and made the *Pon, Pon* signal. He shook his head at me, but he also laughed.

After we arrived and got all of our luggage together we waited for the bus outside the terminal. It finally pulled up and stopped and I could see Aaron heading down the steps. I expected Laci to go running up to him and give him a big hug, but when I glanced at her she was fumbling with her phone instead. I watched her as she studied the screen and pushed buttons; then she smiled broadly and shoved the phone in my face for me to see.

There was a text from Brent and the screen was full of little smiley faces.

"What is that smell?" Jordan asked, wrinkling up his nose as we drove through the city.

"You don't want to know," I told him.

We were going to be staying in the fellowship hall of a local church, unrolling our sleeping bags at night and stuffing all of our things in a corner during the day. On the way there, Aaron asked me and Laci if we wanted to swing by our old house and we told him that we did.

"You lived in a *pink* house?" Tanner asked as we drove by.

"It's not pink," Laci said.

"Yes, it is," Jordan told her. After five years I finally felt vindicated.

All day Monday we worked at the orphanage where we had first met Dorito and then Lily. Dorito was unusually subdued for the entire day and Laci worried that he was coming down with something. I had to admit that I'd been expecting him to be wide open while we were there.

At the fellowship hall that night Laci tucked him into his sleeping bag and then she lay down next to him, kissed him, and then felt his forehead to see if he had a fever. I had the feeling that something else was going on.

When we'd first met Dorito we'd had no idea that one day we would be adopting him so we'd taught him to call us Dave and Laci. He'd had a hard time saying "Dave" (when he tried it sounded a lot more like "Day") and before long he was calling me "Day-Day" all the time. That worked out just fine since I'd had a hard time saying "Doroteo" and turned him into "Dorito".

Fair is fair.

But once we'd decided to adopt him, we'd told him that he could call us Mommy and Daddy if he wanted to . . . and he did. That's why when we went to the orphanage on Monday and he called me "Day-Day" for the first time in two years, I knew that something was up.

Dorito was smart . . . *very* smart, so I just lay down on the other side of him and asked him.

"Are you worried about something, Dorito?"

"When are we going home?"

"Six more days." I held out six fingers to him. "Is that okay? Can you hang out here for six more days?"

"I just don't want to live there anymore."

"Live where? The orphanage?"

He nodded and Laci and I looked at each other.

"No," I said looking back down at him and brushing my thumb across his cheek. "I don't want you to live there anymore either."

When Laci and I'd adopted him we'd started bringing him to our house (the *pink* one) more and more. Very gradually he'd gotten used to the idea that he was a part of our family, but anytime he'd wanted to spend the night at the orphanage we'd let him. Our thought was that we hadn't wanted him to go through the trauma of being suddenly yanked out of the orphanage.

"You need to stay with me and Mommy all the time now," I told him.

"Except when I go to Grandma's?"

"Right."

"And Aunt Jessica's?"

"Right."

"And Charlotte's?

"Uh-huh."

"And Tan-man's?"

"Right," I laughed.

"So," he said, clarifying, "I'm not going to live at the orphanage ever again?"

"Nope. You aren't going to even *go* there unless Mommy and I are with you."

"Because you adopted me."

"And because we love you," Laci said.

"And because you're all ours," I said.

He'd been abandoned in the park when he was about a year and a half old and he *knew* that.

"I just don't want to live there anymore," he said, one more time.

"I don't want you to live there anymore either," I said again. "We're not going to ever leave you, Dorito. You're always going to be ours. *Always.*"

He'd heard this a million times, but I guess he needed to hear it once more. He nodded at me.

"We're supposed to go back there for dinner every night this week though and on Christmas day we're supposed to spend the whole day there playing again. Do you want to do that?"

I decided that if he didn't I'd kick around Mexico City with him.

"Yeah," he said, nodding again. "I'm going to teach Miranda how to play crazy eights."

Tuesday we went to a home church and the kids from the landfill were brought there on the bus. Just like the day before with the orphanage kids, we started teaching the kids how to sign the Christmas carols we'd learned and told them the Christmas story. We fed them and sang to them and got to know them a little bit so that they'd recognize us at the landfill the next day.

We'd already prepped everyone in the youth group as best we could for what it was going to be like at the landfill and what we were going to do. When we pulled up the next day the children spotted the bus and ran to meet us. Some of us got out and started passing out food, while others carried boxes of food out into the landfill to reach those who couldn't (or wouldn't) come to the bus. That's what Jordan and Tanner did.

You may think that I didn't go with them because I didn't want to go down into the landfill (which I didn't), but that's not why. The reason I didn't go with them is because something told me to let them go by themselves . . . that I didn't need to be a part of whatever was going to happen.

When it was time to leave everybody trudged back onto the bus. Dorito had always spent a lot of time at the landfill with Laci – to him it was just another place to play with friends. He bounced up to Tanner and asked if he could sit with him and when Tanner smiled slightly and nodded, Dorito climbed into his lap. Tanner wrapped his arms around Dorito and laid his cheek on the top of Dorito's head,

161

looking out the window quietly. Dorito must have sensed something in Tanner because he didn't talk for most of the ride back to the church.

Jordan sat down looking shell-shocked. I sat down next to him because we'd gotten a phone call while they'd been down at the landfill.

"Jordan?"

"What?" he asked very quietly. He was staring out his window too.

"I wanted to tell you . . . before you heard it from someone else."

"What?" he asked even quieter, his eyes not leaving the window.

"My mom called," I said, as the bus engine came to life.

No reaction.

"Charlotte had her baby."

He kept staring out the window.

"Jordan? Did you hear me?"

"I heard you."

"They're good . . . Charlotte's fine and the baby's healthy."

"Good."

"She had a boy . . ."

He nodded.

"I just thought you'd want to know."

He was still looking out the window, but he nodded again.

The bus lurched forward and I got back up and went to the front where Laci was sitting, leaving Jordan alone with his thoughts.

~ ~ ~

THE DAY AFTER we returned home Mrs. White invited us over for dinner to hear about our trip. We stopped in to see Ashlyn and Brent's new baby on the way over.

Andrew, as Laci's phone full of smiley faces had indicated, was healthy as could be.

All those months of worry for nothing.

Amelia was in 'big sister' mode, carting toys out of her room and lining them up on the couch, presenting him with a new one every time he squealed or hiccupped.

"I can tell you're a big help to your mommy, aren't you?" Laci asked. She nodded dramatically.

Charlotte, on the other hand, had left the hospital without her baby boy. He had gone home with his new parents.

Charlotte had gone home with her mother.

Dorito chattered endlessly throughout dinner, talking all about his friends at the orphanage and the landfill. Charlotte looked up at him when she had to ("And guess *what*, Charlotte?"), but most of the time she stared quietly at her food.

After supper, while Mrs. White went into the kitchen to get dessert, Dorito begged Charlotte to take him to the basement to play foosball.

"I don't think so, Dorito," she said softly, shaking her head.

"You go ahead on down," I told him. "Daddy'll come down and play with you in a few minutes."

Dorito sighed and headed for the stairs, his shoulders sagging in disappointment. Mrs. White returned as he was leaving and Charlotte asked to be excused.

"I can tell it's been hard . . ." Laci said quietly when Charlotte had left. Mrs. White looked through the doorway where she had disappeared and then sat down, looking at the dessert she'd just brought in.

"He looked just like Greg," Mrs. White finally said in a voice barely above a whisper. "Especially his hair."

She glanced at me and then went on, tears spilling out of her eyes. She turned toward Laci who took her hand. "I remember Greg had exactly the same kind of hair when he was born . . ."

Laci squeezed her hand. I pushed my chair back and headed out the door.

Down the hall and to the left was Charlotte's bedroom. Her door was open, but I knocked anyway.

"Can I come in?"

She was sitting on the edge of her bed. She looked up and gave me a little shrug.

I sat down beside her on the bed. I was going to tell her that everything was going to be okay . . . that somewhere out there a family was feeling *so* blessed to have that baby . . . just like Laci and I had been blessed with Dorito and Lily . . . that I knew she was hurting right now though . . . that I was sorry . . . that everything was going to be alright.

I was going to tell her all that, but as soon as I put my arm around her shoulder she started sobbing and she buried her head against me. I wound up just holding her while she cried and I didn't tell her anything that I'd planned on saying.

But I think she knew.

~ ~ ~

TWO MONTHS LATER our combined youth group attended the annual True Love Waits conference that I'd taken Jordan to a year before.

I was more than a little surprised when I found out that Charlotte was planning to attend. I went again too, and I'll go ahead and admit that by now I had a much better attitude about the whole "wait until you're married" idea.

One of the testimonies was given by a young man who said that he'd made poor decisions in the past . . . that he had not remained abstinent, but that he now wished he had. I thought he was going to go on about repercussions, which of course Charlotte already knew *all* about, but he didn't. Instead, he talked to the audience about something called "second virginity".

"In Colossians, Paul tells us that God 'has rescued us from the dominion of darkness and brought us into the kingdom of the Son He loves, in whom we have redemption, the forgiveness of sins.' So what does that mean if you've already done something that you wish you could take back? It means that God offers second chances. It means that He has offered us the gift of forgiveness even though we don't deserve it.

"Just because you've been sexually active in the past doesn't mean that you can't make a commitment to stay sexually abstinent until marriage from this point forward. When you do this, you experience a second virginity. This second virginity comes by asking for God's forgiveness through Jesus and by committing to stay sexually abstinent until marriage.

"Sin *does* have consequences and you may be dealing with some of those consequences now, but by reclaiming your purity, you can have a whole new outlook and freedom in your life."

I'm sure they'd talked about this at the conference the year before too, but I probably hadn't been paying all that much attention. Now, however, I couldn't help but glance toward Charlotte to see if she was.

Not only was she paying attention, but it was obvious that she'd known about all this before signing up for the trip.

After lunch, when she took her pledge, I thought how sorry I was that Jordan wasn't there to see it.

AFTER THE TRUE Love Waits conference, Charlotte slowly began to change. She went back to work at *Wilma's*, and any Saturday when we were out doing something, Tanner and I made it a point to stop in for breakfast.

"Charlotte!" Tanner called out to her one morning.

"What?"

"Where's my sausage?" he asked, pointing to his plate.

She looked at our order slip.

"You didn't order any sausage," she said.

"Yes, I did," Tanner insisted.

"Oh," she said, biting her lip. "Sorry. I'll go get you some."

Four weeks later though he told her that she forgot to put cheese on his hash browns.

"You didn't order any cheese," she told him.

"Yes, I did."

"No," she said, shoving the order slip in his face. "You didn't. If you had ordered cheese on your hash browns I would have written 'cheese' after the words 'hash browns'. Do you see the word 'cheese' on here anywhere?"

"I ordered cheese."

"Do you want cheese?" she asked, putting a hand on her hip.

Tanner nodded at her.

"Fine!" she said, stalking away.

"I don't think you ordered cheese," I whispered after she was gone.

"I know," he smiled at me.

She marched back up to our table and threw a cold slice of cheese down on top of his hash browns.

"It's not melted!" Tanner cried.

"I *know* you didn't say you wanted *melted* cheese," Charlotte said, turning to walk away.

"Hey, Charlotte?" I called, winking at Tanner.

"What?" she sighed, turning around.

"I wanted scrambled," I said, pointing to my fried eggs.

"You want scrambled?"

"Uh-huh."

She marched back to our table and took my fork out of my hand and started chopping my eggs up and mixing them around on my plate.

"There," she said, handing me back my fork. "Now they're scrambled."

It had taken awhile, but our old Charlotte had finally returned.

I was really glad to have her back

When we left Tanner ordered two sausage biscuits to go and Charlotte wrapped them up for him and put them into a paper bag.

"I left your tip on the table," I told her.

"Great," she said. "Now I can retire."

We walked back out to the truck.

"Here," Tanner said, tossing the bag into the backseat where Jordan was sitting.

"We're not choosing between the two of you," I had told him when he'd realized that Tanner was pulling into the parking lot of *Wilma's.* *"You can sit out here and sulk or you can come in and have breakfast."*

He had decided to sit out there and sulk.

Now he glowered at us and took a sip of the slushy that he had managed to walk into the gas station to get while he was waiting.

~ ~ ~

GRADUATION NIGHT CAME and Laci's parents kept Dorito and Lily for us. We sat next to Mrs. White, fanning ourselves with our programs, waiting for the commencement exercises to start. According to the program, Charlotte would be speaking second. The senior class president spoke first, followed by the salutatorian, and finally the valedictorian.

Salutatorian was nothing to sneeze at.

The class president talked for about five minutes . . . I have no idea what about. When it was Charlotte's turn she walked to the podium and adjusted her tassel. Then she looked to her audience and began speaking.

"I believe I'm the only member of our graduating class who has already stood on this stage once before and received a high school diploma. I remember that I was eight years old and I didn't know what a diploma was. My mom explained to me that it was a piece of paper that showed you had gone to high school and learned everything you were supposed to learn. As many of you know, my father and my brother were killed a little over ten years ago. The principal wanted me and my mother to accept my brother's diploma. Even though he didn't get to finish high school, I guess they figured that he had learned everything that he was supposed to have learned.

"So now I stand here again, about to receive my own diploma. Apparently I have also learned what I was supposed to have learned. What exactly, I wonder, is that?

"One thing I've just *recently* learned is that if you're going to make a speech at a public high school graduation, it must be approved by the administration first.

"I was going to tell you one of the things I've learned is that no matter how dismal things may seem, God is always good and He always loves us more than we'll ever know. But Principal Fischer told

169

us that we need to leave God out of our speeches. Apparently the School Board gets edgy when kids start mentioning how good God is or how much He loves us."

She glanced over at Principal Fischer and smiled.

"And I don't want to get him in trouble or anything, so I'm not going to mention all that."

Principal Fischer laughed.

Smooth, Charlotte. Real smooth.

"I decided that I wanted to take this opportunity tonight to share with you some of the most important things that I have learned – but don't panic. I'm not going to be talking to you about Longfellow, or parabolas, or ancient wars, because I'm not going to be talking about things that I've learned in school.

"Although school is all about learning, life is where the *real* learning takes place. Sometimes people make mistakes and those mistakes are usually the most powerful learning experiences that we can have. Any of us can pick up a book and learn the things that are in it, or have a teacher explain to us certain things that we must memorize and then recite back. But the things we learn that matter the *most* along the way are not things that can be put into books. Often they are things that we cannot even share with each other, because they are lessons that can only occur through the unique experiences we each have.

"A biology book can help us determine if a plant is a monocot or a dicot, but it cannot tell us which seeds will grow when they are planted and which ones will not.

"An economics teacher can help us to earn tremendous amounts of money during our lifetime, but he doesn't teach us that the person who chases after money will never have enough.

"In debate class we learn to construct powerful arguments that can sway an audience to agree with a point that even we ourselves may not agree with, but we learn the hard way that once words leave our mouths we can never take them back."

170

As Charlotte spoke I realized that these were thinly veiled passages from Ecclesiastes. I doubted if the atheists in the audience were going to recognize that though.

"We're swamped with articles in magazines and newspapers that share with us the latest research on diet and exercise so that we can live long and healthy lives. I agree that it's important to learn to take care of our bodies, but we would do well to remember that they will only be able to serve us for a limited amount of time, no matter how we treat them. If only we put as much time and thought into preparing for that moment when our bodies will inevitably fail us."

Even the atheists were going to be able to figure out what she was talking about there . . .

"I still have a lot to learn . . . both in school and in life, but one thing I know that's the most important thing for us to learn is how to love. That is why we're here . . . it is the reason we were created."

She was really skating on thin ice now, but she probably figured the superintendent of schools wasn't going to dart across the stage and tackle her mid-speech or anything.

"When I was eight years old I thought that the most painful thing in the world was to lose somebody that you love, but I've since learned that this isn't true. The most painful thing in the world is to *hurt* somebody that you love."

It wasn't my imagination . . . she was looking *straight at* Jordan when she said that.

"I have also learned, however, that the most wonderful thing in the world is to have someone in your life who loves you enough to be able to forgive you after you do hurt them. I have been blessed enough to have people in my life who love me that much.

"Oops," she said, looking over at Principal Fischer again. "I probably shouldn't have said *blessed*."

He smiled at her.

"One last thing I have learned is that each day is a precious gift and that tomorrow is not promised to any of us. Because of that I

171

will tell you *now* that I care for each of you and that I love you and that I'm glad we've shared these years together. And I know I'm not supposed to say this, but I don't care. I pray that God will bless each and every one of you. Thank you."

Before she escaped with her friends to celebrate, I found Charlotte and I hugged her and I told her how proud I was of her and I told her that I loved her. I looked around for Jordan because I wanted to tell him the same thing, but I couldn't find him.

He was already gone.

~ ~ ~

GREG AND HIS father had been killed during a lock-down at our high school, right before Christmas of our senior year. The young man who had killed them was named Kyle Dunn and he had been executed not long before Laci and I were married.

It had been a long process for me to forgive Kyle for what he'd done. Every time I thought that I'd completely forgiven him I would find out that I really hadn't and time and time again God would work through someone to show me that.

One of the first people He'd used had been Greg's mom.

She'd asked me to come over to her house. She'd made me promise her that I would go and visit Kyle in prison. At the time I had honestly thought that she'd been doing it for *Kyle's* sake.

"*David,*" she'd said, looking into my eyes and laying a hand on mine. "*Have I ever asked you to do anything for me?*"

I'd shaken my head at her.

"*I'm asking you now. I want you to please go see Kyle over your Christmas break. Will you do that? Will you do that for me . . . please?*"

I had waited for a long moment and then I'd finally nodded.

"*Promise me.*"

I'd nodded again.

"*I need to hear you say it.*"

"*I promise.*"

"*Promise what?*"

"*I promise I'll go see Kyle . . .*"

She'd looked at me, wanting me to say more, but I had just stared at her.

"*Over Christmas break?*"

I'd nodded again.

"Say it," she'd insisted. *"Over Christmas break."*

I'd nodded one more time and answered. *"Over Christmas break."*

Two weeks after graduation, Charlotte flew to Florida with her mom to visit her grandmother. When she got back there would be only four weeks left before she went off to State and before Jordan went off to Houston. When I realized this and I thought about how Mrs. White had convinced me that I needed to go and forgive Kyle, I knew what I had to do and I wandered across the street.

Jordan was in the shop, running on the treadmill. The sweat was pouring off of him.

"Hey, David. What's up?" he asked, pushing a button on the treadmill. He slowed down to a jog, and then came to a complete stop.

"I just wanted to talk to you about something for a minute," I said, sitting down on the weight bench.

"Okay," he nodded, reaching for his water bottle. He took a few long swigs and leaned back against a handrail of the treadmill, breathing heavily and looking at me expectantly.

I finally decided to just get right to it.

"I want you to go and talk to Charlotte when she gets back from Florida."

He turned away from me, put his water bottle back in its holder, and started jogging again.

"You know, Jordan," I said over the noise of the treadmill. "Everybody makes mistakes."

"Tell me about it."

"You've made mistakes . . ."

"Yeah," he admitted, running harder. "But I haven't managed to get *pregnant* yet."

174

"You have to forgive her Jordan."

"No, I don't."

"Yes, you do."

"I don't owe her anything," he said, his feet pounding away.

"I didn't say that you owe her anything. Charlotte doesn't need you to forgive her . . . she's going to be fine whether you forgive her or not. You need to forgive for *you*, not for her . . ."

"I'm fine," he said, dismissing me with his hand. "I've forgiven her. I'm fine."

He managed to run even faster . . . he was driving me nuts. I reached over to the treadmill and pulled out the safety key, causing it to grind to a stop.

"You haven't forgiven her!" I cried. "If you'd forgiven her you'd be able to talk about her . . . you could stand to be in the same room with her . . . you could go and *tell her* that you've forgiven her."

He glared at me.

David . . . have I ever asked you to do anything for me? I'm asking you now. I want you to please go see Kyle over your Christmas break. Will you do that? Will you do that for me . . . please?

"Jordan," I said, "have I ever asked you to do anything before?"

"Um, yeah," he nodded, wiping his face with a towel. "You asked me to go minister to a bunch of kids who live in a landfill in Mexico."

"Okay, fine, Jordan. Just fine! Go off to college this fall mad at Charlotte – see if I care." I was yelling at him now. "You're all the time telling me how you want to pay me back for everything, but then when I come over here and ask you for *one thing* you can't do it for me. Thanks a lot."

I got off the weight bench and headed for the door, but before I stepped down into the yard I turned around and faced him one more time.

"You know, Jordan, you always talk about how you want to do what God wants you to do. Until right now I always thought you actually meant that."

I stepped down into the yard and was almost to the corner of the house when I heard him.

"I'll tell her."

I turned around and looked at him. He had followed me to the doorway of the shop and was standing there, looking at me.

"You will?"

He nodded.

Promise me. I need to hear you say it.

I promise.

Promise what?

I promise I'll go see Kyle . . .

Over Christmas break? Say it . . . over Christmas break.

Over Christmas break.

"You promise?" I asked him.

He nodded again.

"Say it."

"I promise."

I decided that was good enough.

~ ~ ~

THE NEXT DAY I was in my office working when Laci called from the living room.

"David!"

"What?"

"Come here!"

I went into the living room.

Laci was standing there with the remote in her hand, pointed at the noon news which was frozen on the screen.

"What?" I asked again.

"Watch this," she said, hitting play.

"Authorities say that a body was discovered in the trunk of a submerged car found yesterday at Cross Lake . . ." the anchor woman said as footage of a car being towed from the water played on the screen. *"License plates and registration tags indicate the vehicle may have been underwater for six years, but further details are not being released at this time."*

"So?" I said.

"Don't you recognize that car?" she asked me, rewinding and hitting play again.

I looked at the car. It did look familiar . . . familiar enough that I knew what she was thinking, but . . .

"David!" she said. "That's Tanner's dad's car!"

"Naw," I said, shaking my head at her while at the same time thinking that it did look an awful lot like the car I'd learned to drive straight-drive in . . .

"Yes it is, David. Yes it is! I went to the prom with Tanner in that car! He drove you and me home from the state championship game in that car! It's Tanner's dad's car . . . you *know* it is!"

I kept shaking my head at her, but the whole time all I could think of was that she was absolutely right.

177

~ ~ ~

BY THE NEXT day, dental records had confirmed that the body in the trunk was that of Tanner and Jordan's father. The official cause of death was a single gunshot wound to the head and the body was released to the family one week after it had been discovered. It was strange to have a funeral service for a man who had been dead for six years . . . a man whom everyone previously had assumed had disappeared of his own volition.

Following the service we went to a local cemetery and after the burial I talked with Jordan and Tanner's middle brother, Chase, for a few minutes. It had been a long time since I'd seen him because he lived just outside of Chicago now and I told him that it was good to see him again and I told him how sorry I was.

After that I scanned the graveyard and saw Mike, standing alone at his own father's grave. Danica hadn't come with him. I walked over to him and stood a few yards away until he spotted me.

"Hi . . ." he said.

"You doing all right?"

"Yeah," he nodded and looked back down at the grave as I took a few steps closer.

"Do you come here a lot?" I asked.

"No," Mike said, shaking his head. He looked back up at me and gave me a slight smile. "He's not here . . ."

He's not here . . .

I gave him a smile back.

~ ~ ~

THREE DAYS LATER I was in the backyard with Dorito when Jordan appeared from around the side of the house.

"Hi," he said, climbing the deck steps.

"Hi Jordan!" Dorito yelled from his swing.

"Hi, Dorito."

"How are you doing?" I asked him as he sat down. I hadn't seen him since the funeral.

"I don't know," he answered, shaking his head. He stared out into the backyard and watched Dorito swing.

After a moment Laci stepped out onto the deck and walked over to him. She leaned over and wrapped her arms around him and held him for a minute and then she kissed the top of his head.

She rubbed his shoulder and then called to Dorito.

"What?"

"Come on in and get a popsicle."

"Are there any red ones?"

"Yep."

"Yeaaa!"

He jumped off the swing and raced onto the deck, stopping for a moment in front of Jordan.

"I get to have a red popsicle!"

"I know," Jordan said, trying to smile. "I heard."

"Yummy!"

Laci held the door open for him and then closed it behind her, leaving me and Jordan alone.

Jordan sat staring out at the swing that was still swaying slightly back and forth. I was pretty sure I knew exactly what was going through his mind. Even though his dad had been gone for six years, a part of him had probably always hoped that one day . . .

"I lied to the police," Jordan said.

On the other hand, maybe I had absolutely no *idea what was going through his mind.*

"Huh?"

He nodded. "I lied to the police."

"About what?"

"They asked me if I had any idea what happened."

"And what'd you tell them?"

"I told them no."

"How's that a lie?"

"Because," he said. "I think I know who killed my dad."

"*You do?*"

He nodded again.

"Who?"

I saw tears well up in his eyes and then he put his head down on his hands and started sobbing.

"Jordan," I said, sliding my chair over toward his so I could put my hand on his shoulder. "What's going on? Who do you think killed your dad?"

Although he was crying pretty hard he finally choked out a response.

"Tanner," he said. "I think Tanner did it."

I almost pulled my hand off of his shoulder in disbelief, but managed to shake his shoulder instead and then I patted him on the back and tried to calm him down.

"Jordan . . . *what* are you talking about?"

"I'm talking about *Tanner*. I think Tanner killed my dad and stuffed his body in the trunk and then drove it into Cross Lake . . . *that's* what I'm talking about."

"Why in the *world* would you think that?"

"Because," Jordan said, trying to compose himself a bit. "Everything fits . . . *everything*."

"Like what?"

"The week my dad disappeared I was at a baseball training camp in Oklahoma," Jordan began. He was calming down now . . . as if he were really glad to be finally talking about it with someone.

"When I came home Mom told me that Dad had left. 'Course I was upset, but I really wasn't all that surprised. I mean, they'd been fighting all the time and I'd already heard Mom talking about leaving him . . . I just kinda figured he'd gotten outta there first."

"Okay . . ."

"But there were some things that didn't really make sense. Like if he was going to move out, why wouldn't he take his sunglasses . . . his toothbrush . . . his favorite jacket? I mean that didn't seem right, but I was only ten years old, so I really didn't put a whole lot of thought into it . . ."

"I don't really see how—"

"But then one day I go down in the basement to look for a donut for my bat. At camp they'd had us use 'em and I thought I'd remembered seeing one down there so I thought I'd go look around for it, ya know?"

"Uh-huh."

"So I go down there and everything's . . . *different*."

"Different how?"

"Like . . . all cleaned up."

"So your mom cleaned . . ."

"No," he said, shaking his head. "Not cleaned up like that. Just . . ."

"Just what?"

"Everything was all rearranged and shuffled around. If she'd been cleaning it would have been neat and organized, but it wasn't."

"Yeah, but—"

"And everything had been *bleached* . . . the cement floor, the walls . . . I mean it smelled like bleach down there for weeks after I got home."

I just looked at him.

181

"I didn't think a whole lot about that either at the time, but that's where it happened," he nodded with certainty. "Somebody killed him there and then they cleaned it all up."

"Well, what makes you think it was *Tanner?*"

"My mom and I went over to his place to tell him about it after the police told us. He didn't even act surprised. I mean, he was *upset* . . . but he wasn't surprised."

"Well," I said. "Maybe he saw the footage on TV . . ."

"Ya ever notice how Tanner never wants to go to Cross Lake?"

Maybe . . .

"What reason could he *possibly* have for going to Makasoi all the time?" Jordan continued.

"I don't know, but–"

"Maybe because it gives him the creeps to fish in the same lake where he dumped our dad's body?"

"Oh, come on, Jordan . . ."

"Well who else could have done it?" he cried.

"Anybody! Anybody could have done it!"

"Well, who else would have cleaned up with *bleach* in the basement?"

"I . . . I don't know," I stammered. "Your mom?"

Oh, that's real good, David. Make him think his mom did it. That's bound to make him feel loads better.

"No," he said, shaking his head. "My mom and Chase went to my grandmother's in Missouri that week to help her paint her house . . . that's why Chase didn't go to baseball camp with me. My dad was the only one home . . . and Tanner was less than an hour away at school. It *had* to be Tanner."

"There's no way Tanner killed your father. There's got to be a logical explanation."

"Like what?"

"I . . . I don't know, Jordan. Why don't you just ask him about it?"

"You mean like 'Hey, Tanner? I've been wondering . . . did you kill Dad?' Yeah, David . . . that sounds like a *great* plan!"

"Just go talk to him . . . I'm sure you'll see how ridiculous you're being . . ."

But Jordan just shook his head at me and stared back out at the swing set again.

"Do you want me to talk to him?" I finally asked quietly.

Jordan looked at me and nodded.

~ ~ ~

AS I DROVE over to Tanner's that afternoon I tried to sort it all out. I thought about everything Jordan had said and I tried to get the image out of my mind of Tanner stuffing his dad's body into the trunk of the car and then driving it into the lake.

There was no way he could've done it . . . *no way*.

I could hardly wait to get there so he could explain to me how there was no way.

~ ~ ~

"HI," TANNER SAID, opening his front door.

"Hey. Am I catching you at a bad time?"

"No . . . not really."

"Can I come in?"

"Sure."

I stepped into his living room.

"You want something to drink?"

"Uh, no. I'm good."

"You wanna sit down?

"Yeah."

"So what's up?" he asked, sitting down opposite me.

"Ummm . . . Jordan came by this morning."

"Oh?"

"Yeah . . . he was pretty upset."

"It hasn't been easy . . ." Tanner said, shaking his head.

"Yeah, well . . . listen," I said, rubbing my eyes. "He was like twelve when your dad disappeared . . . you know . . . he was just a kid."

"Yeah . . . so?"

"Well, you know . . . a kid that age can have a really big imagination . . ."

"What are you talking about?"

"Well, he just . . . I don't know . . . he saw some things when he was little and he's just got a lot of questions and he was so upset that I told him I'd come over and talk to you."

"Questions? What kind of questions?"

"Well, he's convinced that somebody killed your dad in the basement and then cleaned it all up and everything and . . . I don't know . . . he's just got himself all upset . . ."

Tanner's eyes narrowed.

"My dad's dead. Talking about this isn't going to bring him back."

"I know, but . . ."

"I need you to just drop this."

"But he . . . he was *murdered.*"

"I said you need to drop this."

"But—"

"Listen, David . . . I'm asking you as a friend . . . you're my friend right?"

"Of course I am," I said.

"Because what I need right now is for you to be my friend."

"You know I'm your friend . . ."

"Then I need you to forget about this."

"But—"

"Please? Just stop it. Okay? Please?"

Be supportive . . . be a good friend.

I looked at him for a long moment and then gave him a little nod.

"Okay . . ." I managed.

"Good."

He stood up. Apparently our conversation was over. I stood up too and he walked me to the door. I opened it, stepped down onto the porch, and turned to face him again.

I just couldn't leave well enough alone.

"Tanner," I said again, looking up at him. "I don't understand what the big deal is. Just tell me what's going on . . . or at *least* tell Jordan . . . I mean he thinks that you *killed* his father!"

Tanner looked at me for a moment.

"Is that what you think?" he finally asked.

And do you know what I did?

I hesitated.

Not for long. Just long enough to wonder again why Tanner always refused to go fishing at Cross Lake. Just long enough for that

186

image of Tanner killing his father and stuffing his body into the trunk of that car to flash through my mind one more time. Just long enough for Tanner to know that I'd actually *considered* that he might have done it.

"You know what, David?" he asked, glaring at me with a look on his face I'd never seen before. "You can go to Hell."

And then he slammed the door in my face.

~ ~ ~

I THINK THE best word to use to describe me after that was probably *despondent.*

I refused to tell Laci what was going on. All she knew was that I'd had a fight with Tanner, but she had no idea what about.

I'd never before felt so burdened about anything in my entire life and I wasn't about to have her feeling the same way. I wished that Jordan had never told me.

What was I supposed to do? At what point did I stop being supportive and stop being a good friend? Shouldn't I call the police and tell them what I knew? Wasn't it a *felony* to withhold information? How long was I supposed to just keep my mouth shut and pretend like everything was fine?

"Why don't you go see Mike?" Laci asked quietly the next day. She'd been a lot more understanding than I thought she would be when I explained to her that I didn't want to tell her anything, but that didn't stop her from worrying about me or trying to help.

"Because I'm not running to Mike every time I have a problem," I snapped.

"I'm sorry," she said quietly. "I just thought maybe you could use a friend."

Not only was I not going to burden *her* with this . . . I wasn't going to burden Mike with it either.

But Laci was right about one thing . . .

I could use a friend.

~ ~ ~

FOR THE SECOND time in a week I found myself at a cemetery. I stopped first at Gabby's grave which had fresh flowers on it. I didn't know who had put them there. My mom . . . Laci's mom . . . Laci . . . Mrs. White? They all came here a lot, so it could've been any one of them. I on the other hand hardly *ever* came here because when I did, it just made me feel like crying.

After I'd visited Gabby's grave I walked over to where Mr. White and Greg were buried. I looked down at Mr. White's grave before I moved to Greg's and then I stood there for a long time.

He's not here . . .

Finally I sat down.

"Hi," I said and I glanced around the cemetery to make sure I was alone. I looked back at Greg's grave.

"You wouldn't believe how messed up everything is," I told him. I shook my head and looked up at the sky. After a while I looked back down to his grave.

"I don't know what to do," I finally said, my voice starting to break. "I don't know what to do . . ."

The tears started coming and I knew I wasn't going to be able to stop them. I put my elbows on my knees and buried my face into my hands and I cried and I cried.

That's why I hardly ever came here.

~ ~ ~

I ASKED GOD to show me what to do. He didn't tell me to go talk to Tanner. He didn't tell me to go to the police. He just told me that I should pray for Tanner.

Of course I'd *been* praying for Tanner all along, but perhaps not with as much fervor as I did now.

I tried to be unselfish when I prayed, but what I really wanted to pray about was my relationship with Tanner. All I *should* have prayed about was Tanner's relationship with God, and that's what I tried to stick to, but it was really hard.

In the meantime, Jordan and I managed to spend the next week completely avoiding each other. Of course I wasn't about to walk over to his house and tell him that he was right – that it did indeed look as if Tanner might have killed their father. And when I didn't come over, Jordan must have figured out that whatever news I had wasn't good.

Our ten year class reunion took place eight days after Tanner had slammed the door in my face. We'd sent in our money weeks ago and Laci was excited, but I dreaded going and sulked about it whenever I had the chance.

"It's going to be fun, David!" Laci insisted as we were getting ready to go.

"No," I said. "It's not going to be fun."

"Don't you want to go and see all of your friends?"

"*ALL OF MY FRIENDS?*" I cried. "Are you kidding, Laci? I'm not going to have any friends there!"

She looked at me doubtfully, but she didn't make me remind her that Mike had graduated the year after us, Greg was dead, and Tanner hated my guts.

"Brent's going to be there . . ."

"Oh, come on, Laci," I said. "The only reason I even *talk* to Brent is because he's married to Ashlyn. I don't have one thing in common with him."

"But he's nice . . ."

"I never said he wasn't nice."

"You know what, David?"

"What?" I asked, not really wanting to know.

"Every time you go to something like this you sit around and mope and don't talk to anybody and you don't even *try* to have meaningful conversations . . ."

"How are you supposed to have a meaningful conversation with somebody that you haven't seen in ten years? That's why I hate stuff like this, Laci. You've got to go around giving obligatory hugs to everybody you see and making small talk all evening. *I hate it.*"

"Maybe you can hug your old girlfriend!" Laci teased. "I'll bet you could find something to talk with her about!"

"Ughh," I said. "I can't think of anything more awkward than running into Sam tonight. Now I *really* don't want to go."

"Well," she said. "I'm looking forward to seeing everybody . . ."

"Of course you are. You're going to have Natalie and Ashlyn to visit with all evening."

"Even if Natalie and Ashlyn *weren't* going to be there I'd still wanna go. Unlike *you* I know how to have meaningful conversations with people."

"Oh," I said, waving my hand dismissively at her. "I know how to have meaningful conversations . . ."

"I'll bet you couldn't have one meaningful conversation all evening . . ."

"I could too . . ."

"Not with somebody you wouldn't normally talk to," she challenged.

"Oh, baloney. I could have meaningful conversations all night long."

"Prove it!" she said. "Come on. You wanna bet? Let's make a bet! I'll bet you can't even talk to *three* people that you wouldn't normally talk to."

She was just hoping to take my mind off my troubles.

"Come on! What do you want if you win? Let's hear it!"

Poor Laci. She was trying so hard to cheer me up. I knew she was wanting me to raise an eyebrow at her and smile.

You know what I want . . .

But all I really wanted was for Jordan to forgive Charlotte. I wanted for Tanner to be my friend again and I wanted to not think that he might have killed his father.

"I don't want anything," I finally said. "We can bet if you want to, but I don't want anything if I win."

We arrived fairly early at the convention center and parked. We walked down the circular drive, around a big fountain, and toward the main doors where a man in a tuxedo held the door open for us. The convention center was huge with several ballrooms . . . our reunion wasn't the only event being held there. A sign indicated there were two wedding receptions and a business convention going on as well. Our reunion was in the Fleetwood Ballroom at the end of the vast lobby.

Outside the ballroom was a table to check-in at and seated behind it were our class officers.

"Hannah!" Laci cried out to one of them. Hannah had been our class treasurer. She stood up and hugged Laci. It had started already.

192

"Hi, David!" Hannah said, giving me an obligatory hug. She checked our names off on her list, handed each of us name tags, and grabbed two booklets from a pile in front of her.

"Here you go," she said. "Calen made these for everyone." She pointed to the person sitting next to her. Calen had been our vice president.

"Oh!" Laci said. "Calen!"

More hugs . . .

We went into the ballroom and started looking around. It didn't take Laci long to spot Natalie, sitting at a table by herself. Laci ran to the table, but I followed along at a more leisurely pace.

After still more hugs we sat down. The tables each seated eight people. I knew Ashlyn and Brent would get two of the seats, but the other three were up for grabs. I took a moment to feel sorry for myself one more time that none of my friends were going to be sitting there, and then I started looking at the booklet that Calen had made.

She'd copied all of our senior pictures from our yearbook and put everybody's contact information next to it so people wouldn't have to spend all evening exchanging phone numbers. She'd also taken information from a questionnaire that had been mailed to us in the spring that told what everyone was doing for a living and how many kids they had and everything.

Laci stopped talking to Natalie long enough to hit me on the shoulder.

"David!"

"What?" I asked, not looking up.

"You're not doing a very good job with our bet yet. Why don't you get your nose out of that and visit with Natalie?"

"Natalie doesn't count," I said, still not looking up. "I'm supposed to talk to people who I wouldn't normally talk to . . . *remember?* Natalie's my friend . . . she doesn't count."

"So you're going to sit there and ignore her?"

"I'm not ignoring her," I said, turning a page in the booklet. "I've heard every word she's said."

"Liar."

I closed the booklet and looked at Laci.

"Natalie's moving home," I said. "Her father isn't doing too good with his Parkinson's and she thinks her mom's going to be needing a lot of help before too long. The medicine he's on makes him hallucinate, and sometimes the hallucinations are worse than the disease. Last week he refused to go to bed because he was convinced that a bunch of nuns were having a convention in the back yard and her mom was up until three in the morning with him."

I glanced at Natalie. "How'm I doing so far?"

"Pretty good," she smiled.

"What were the nuns holding?" Laci challenged.

"Golf clubs."

Laci sighed and I went on.

"She hates the thought of leaving Denver because she's grown so close to all the kids at her church that she really doesn't want to leave them, but she knows that God's got plans for her and she's just going to be obedient and let Him be in charge. That's about where she was when you started *hitting* me."

"You know," Laci said. "You could be polite and visit with Natalie. You haven't seen her in months . . ."

I sighed heavily and put the booklet down. I propped my elbows on the table and rested my chin on my hands.

"Hi, Natalie!" I said. "How're you doing?"

She laughed.

"I'm great, David."

"*Wonderful!* I'm so glad to hear that. Say! I love your earrings! Where'd you get them?"

"My mother . . ."

"Oh! Interesting . . ." I said, nodding my head. "You know, I've been thinking about getting my ears pierced . . . does it hurt a lot?"

She laughed again.

"Forget it," Laci said. "Sit there and be rude. See if I care."

"Don't worry about it," Natalie assured her. "David's been rude to me for years . . . I'm used to it."

"Like you don't deserve it," I muttered.

"Oh, get over it already!" Natalie cried.

"One thing!" I said, holding a finger toward her face. "I've only ever asked you for *one thing!*"

I remembered we'd been in the fifth grade . . .

Here, Natalie, I'd said, handing her the masterpiece I'd made in art class. *Watch this for me. Don't let anything happen to it. I'll be right back . . .*

"First of all," Natalie was saying, "it was one of the *ugliest* pieces of pottery I've ever seen in my life. Second of all . . . *IT WAS AN ACCIDENT!* How many times do I have to tell you that *it was an accident?!*"

"I can't talk about this anymore," I told Laci. "It's too upsetting. Can I please go back to my reading?"

"Be my guest," Laci said. "I give up."

I winked at Natalie and went back to the booklet. When I got to the last page I read what was at the top.

"I am the resurrection and the life. He who believes in me will live, even though he dies; and whoever lives and believes in me will never die."

Underneath that, it said: *"In loving memory . . ."* and underneath that there were pictures. One of Greg and one of Mr. White, one of a history teacher of ours who'd died from a heart attack, and four of our classmates who had died since we'd graduated. One had been killed in an auto accident, two had died from cancer, and one had committed suicide.

"I'll be right back," I told Laci.

"Where are you going?"

"I'm going to go and have meaningful conversation number one," I told her and I went through the crowds and out toward the lobby. When I got there I walked up to the check-in table.

"Hey, Calen?"

"Yes?"

"You got a second?"

"Sure . . ." She handed a folder of paperwork to Hannah and stood up.

"What can I do for you?" she asked after she'd come around the table.

"I just wanted to thank you for putting this together," I said, holding up the booklet.

"Really?" She looked pleased.

"Yeah. It was a really good idea . . ."

"Well thanks for saying that," she smiled.

I turned it open to the back page and showed it to her.

"Especially this," I said. "I'm really glad you did this . . ."

She looked at it, nodded, and smiled again.

"I'm glad you like it."

"It's not just because of Greg and Mr. White," I said. "Anybody here that was friends with someone who died is going to really appreciate it – even if they don't ever tell you that."

"Thanks."

"And I liked the Scripture too . . ."

She smiled at me.

"Well, I just wanted to thank you," I said. "I didn't mean to drag you away from your job."

"I'm glad you did," she said. "We're about ready to close-up anyway. I think everybody that's coming is pretty much here already. Thanks again." She turned to go.

"Oh! Calen?"

"Yeah?" she turned back toward me.

"Has ummm . . . has Tanner shown up?"

"No," she said. "He sent in his money, but he hasn't checked in yet."

"Oh."

"Take care."

"Bye."

I walked back into the ballroom which was pretty crowded by now. I spotted Laci and Natalie and could see that Ashlyn and Brent had arrived. I started winding my way back toward our table, but stopped and did a double take when I saw Nick. I couldn't figure out why Nick would be at our reunion. We'd been in youth group together and on the swim team together, but he'd graduated a year ahead of me.

"What's up, Nick?" I asked, walking over to him. He was sitting next to some guy I didn't recognize. "Did you get held back a grade or something and I just don't remember?"

"Hey, David!" he smiled, standing up and shaking my hand. "I married Angel. You remember Angel?"

Angel? Samantha's best friend, Angel?

"Sure," I said. "I remember Angel."

"And you remember Samantha?"

Vaguely . . .

"Of course I do . . ."

He indicated the guy sitting next to him.

"This is Sam's husband . . . Mark."

"Hi, Mark," I said, reaching out to shake his hand. "Nice to meet you."

"Nice to meet you too," he said. He looked past me. "Here come the girls . . ."

Of course . . .

I turned around to see Sam and Angel striding toward the table.

Sam's eyes lit up when she saw me.

"David!" she said, hugging me. "It's so good to see you! How are you doing?"

"I'm great . . . how are you?"

"I'm good," she smiled.

"Hi, David," Angel said as she gave me a hug too.

"Nice to see you," I said. "You look great . . . both of you look great."

They smiled at me and then *Laci* appeared at my side with a big grin on her face.

Oh, brother . . .

There was another round of greetings and then Laci looked at me with that huge grin still on her face.

"David!" she said. "I just had a great idea! You and Sam should *dance* together!"

I glared at her.

"Go ahead!" she urged. "It'll give me a chance to catch up with Nick!"

I'm going to kill you, Laci. I'm absolutely going to kill you.

She just blinked her eyes at me innocently and smiled. I was trapped with no options so I turned to Sam.

"Would you like to dance?"

"Sure," she said and we went out onto the dance floor.

"I'll try to make this as painless as possible," she said as she put her arms around my neck.

"Huh?"

"That look you shot her," she said, nodding back toward Laci. "Obviously you'd rather be having your teeth pulled than to dance with me . . ."

"Oh, no . . ." I said, shaking my head. "I'm sorry. That didn't have anything to do with *you* . . ."

She looked at me skeptically.

"I promise," I said, smiling at her. "I'm really glad to see you."

She smiled back.

198

"As a matter of fact," I said, "if your husband wasn't over there I'd dance with you for the rest of the night just to teach Laci a lesson."

"He's a good sport," she grinned.

"How good?"

"Pretty good . . ."

She leaned up and whispered in my ear. "Pretend like I just said something *really* funny," and then she threw her head back and laughed.

I laughed too. Not just because I was trying get even with Laci, but because Sam was fun and I remembered that we'd always had a good time together.

"Well?" she asked, since I was the one facing Laci and I was the one who knew her well enough to be able to tell if we'd gotten to her at all.

We had.

"It's a start," I said, grinning. "Thanks."

"Anytime . . . glad to help."

The song was already ending.

"You want to keep dancing?" she asked.

"Sure," I nodded, glancing toward Laci again. "That'd be good . . ."

"So do you have any kids?"

"Yeah," I answered, reaching for my wallet. I flipped it open to a picture of Dorito holding Lily. "This is Dorito and Lily."

We stopped dancing so she could look at the picture.

"You've adopted!" she said.

"You don't miss a trick, do you?" I teased as I put my wallet away.

"Did you say . . . *Dorito?*"

"It's a nickname," I explained as we started dancing again.

"What made you guys decide to adopt?"

"We had a baby, Gabby, but she was stillborn, and then Laci had three miscarriages and now she can't have children . . ."

"Oh!" she said, looking dismayed. "I'm so sorry to hear that you two went through all that . . ."

I nodded at her.

"But Lily and," she cleared her throat, ". . . *Dorito* look like really great kids."

"Thanks," I smiled. "They are. What about you? Do you have any kids?"

She broke into a huge smile.

"We're expecting our first," she said. "We just found out last week!"

"That's great! Congratulations!" Then I hesitated.

"Oh . . . I'm sorry . . ."

"About what?"

"I don't guess you really want to be hearing about stillborns and miscarriages and stuff right now . . ."

"No, really . . . it's fine. Please don't worry about it."

"So," I said. "Tell me about ol' what's-his-name over there." I nodded my head toward her husband.

"Mark?"

"Yeah."

"He's an engineer."

"Are you serious?"

"Yeah . . . why?"

"*I'm* an engineer."

"Really? What kind?"

"Structural . . ."

"Oh," she said. "Mark's a computer engineer. So am I. That's how we met."

"You're an engineer?"

"Yeah," she said. "Why do you think I took so many math classes?"

200

"I don't remember you wanting to be an engineer."

"I don't remember you wanting to be an engineer either."

"Well," I admitted, "I didn't really know what I wanted to do when I was in high school, but Greg was going to be an engineer and he got me interested in it."

"Oh," she said, and then she was quiet so we just danced for a while.

Finally she looked at me. She opened her mouth and then closed it . . . as if she'd wanted to say something, but had thought better of it.

"What?" I asked her.

"Nothing," she said, shaking her head.

"*What?*"

She hesitated again, but then finally spoke.

"How come Greg hated me?"

"What do you mean?"

"I *mean*," she said, "that Greg hated me and I've always wondered why."

"Greg didn't hate you," I said, laughing and shaking my head, but she nodded her head at me.

"Yes, he did."

"Sam," I assured her. "Trust me . . . he didn't *hate* you."

"Okay . . . he *greatly disliked* me. Is that better?"

"Why do you think that?"

She rolled her eyes at me.

"I'm not blind!" she said. "He'd be standing there talking and laughing with you and then if I came along he couldn't get away from me fast enough!"

I couldn't deny that there was some truth in what she was saying.

"I think what bothers me so much," she went on, "is that after he and his dad got killed all I ever heard about was what a *strong Christian* he was and how *nice* he was to everybody . . . but he wasn't nice to me. I always wondered why somebody who was such a strong *Christian* would treat someone like that."

She stopped dancing. The song was ending, but I had a feeling that she would have stopped anyway and I suddenly realized that I didn't know if she'd been saved or not; we'd never talked about it.

She'd been my *girlfriend* . . . how could I not know? Tanner had been one of my *best friends* . . . how could I not know?

What was wrong with me?

A fast song was starting up and a new wave of people flooded the dance floor.

"Do you want to go out there and talk for a minute?" I asked, pointing toward the lobby.

She nodded at me.

"Do you want to tell Mark first?" I asked.

"No," she said. "He's fine. Do you want to tell Laci?"

"No," I said, because even though I was upset about what she'd just said, in the back of my mind I was thinking that it wouldn't hurt one bit to give Laci a little something to worry about.

I took her arm and guided her to the lobby. We found a vacant pair of chairs and sat down.

"Look, Sam," I said, trying to decide how to word what I needed to say.

"Greg didn't hate you . . . he didn't even dislike you. He just . . . he just thought that Laci and I should be together. That's all. He just thought I should be dating *her*, not you . . . or anyone else for that matter."

"No," Sam said, shaking her head. "He never liked me . . . *never!* Even before you and I started dating."

"Well," I shrugged, "He knew that I liked you before we ever started dating . . ."

"David," she said, tilting her head at me. "He acted like that when we were in junior high school."

202

"Uh-huh . . ." I said, trying not to smile. I bit my lip and looked up at the ceiling.

"Right," she said, looking at me skeptically. "You liked me ever since junior high . . ."

"*Maybe* . . ." I said, not trying to hide my smile this time.

She looked at me for a second to see if I was serious (which I was), laughed, and shook her head.

"You really liked me in junior high?"

I nodded.

"And that's really all it was?" she asked.

"I promise," I said. "I'm really sorry that Greg made you feel like he didn't like you. If he'd realized how he was making you feel, he wouldn't have acted that way and if he were here now I know he'd apologize. He never would have intentionally done anything that might have kept you from . . ."

"From what?" she asked when I hesitated.

"He *was* a strong Christian," I finally said. "That was the most important thing to him . . ."

"And you think I'm not a *Christian?*" she asked in a surprised voice.

"I don't know," I admitted.

"I'm a Christian, David," she assured me. "I mean, I'm not saying I was where I needed to be back then or that I was where I am now, but *trust me* . . . I'm a Christian."

I smiled at her as she went on.

"I know I should just be able to forgive him without talking to you about it and without knowing why he acted that way, but I feel a lot better about it now. I'm glad we talked about it."

"Good. I am too."

"A Christian *and* an engineer," she said, grinning as she stood up. "I bet you're sorry that you dumped me now, aren't you?"

"I didn't dump you!" I protested, standing up also. "You dumped me!"

"Uh-huh."

"You did!"

"No," she corrected me. "I asked you if you thought we should start seeing other people and you *did* want to start seeing other people, didn't you? If you'd said 'no' or acted like you were the least bit upset then maybe we wouldn't have broken up . . . but it was pretty obvious that you had your mind on someone else."

"Maybe . . ."

"There's no *maybe* about it," she smiled. "As a matter of fact, here comes 'someone else' right now."

I turned around and saw Laci walking toward us.

"Quick," I said. "Hug me like you mean it!"

"No problem."

She gave me a big hug.

"Thanks again," she said. "I really am glad that we talked."

"Me too."

She took a few steps toward the ballroom and then turned back to me.

"Don't forget, David," she said very loudly so Laci'd be able to hear her. "If you ever want to give it another try . . ."

"I'll keep it in mind," I grinned. She walked away and I turned to face Laci.

"You two are *very* funny," she said as I smiled at her.

"I know," I said, reaching my hand out to take hers. I sank back down into my chair and pulled her down onto my lap. "Can we go home now?"

"We've only been here for forty-five minutes!" she protested.

"Are you serious?" I looked at my watch. It seemed like it had been a lot longer. I sighed and wrapped my arms around her and she laid her head on my shoulder. I picked up one of her hands, kissed it, and started rubbing it with my thumb. "Well, I'm ready to go home whenever you are."

I didn't really have any hopes of going home this early, but I thought that maybe if she felt sorry enough for me she'd at least sit there a little while and let me hold her.

She did.

After a while I told her about my talks with Calen and with Sam.

"It really bothered me to think that Greg might have done something to keep Sam from being saved," I said after telling her about meaningful conversation number two.

"Sometimes people make mistakes," Laci said.

"I suppose . . ."

"And I know it's easy to remember him like he was a saint or something," she went on, "but he wasn't."

"I suppose," I said again.

"He was close, though." She looked up at me and smiled and I smiled back at her; then she rested her head on my shoulder again. I put my cheek on top of her head and closed my eyes.

We sat there quietly for a few minutes until I felt her squeeze my hand. I squeezed it back, but she jabbed her elbow into my ribs so I opened my eyes.

Tanner was there, standing about ten yards away, looking at us.

Laci stood up and then I did too.

"I'm going back in," she said quietly and I nodded at her. I took a deep breath and started walking toward Tanner, thinking that if he decided to punch me it was probably really going to hurt.

"Hi," he said when I got to him.

"Hi."

"You wanna step outside and get some fresh air?"

Fewer witnesses . . .

"Sure."

We walked out the front doors toward the fountain. It seemed as if there were a hundred people out there smoking.

So much for getting fresh air . . .

We headed for a bench some distance away that was a pick-up/drop-off spot for city bus riders and when we reached it we sat down. Tanner leaned forward and put his elbows on his knees, clasped his hands together in front of him, and looked down at the sidewalk.

He didn't say anything for a long time and for some reason (I don't know why), my mind turned to a time one fall when we were about nine years old and his mom had taken us to an orchard. We'd quickly gotten bored with picking apples so Tanner had taken his baseball bat from the back of their minivan and pretty soon we were pitching wormy apples to each other and making a huge mess.

Sitting next to him now, remembering that day, somehow I suddenly felt very sad.

"After I went to college," he finally said, breaking the silence, "my dad started changing. I mean *really* changing."

He glanced at me to make sure I was listening before he went on.

"I had summer classes and training and stuff, so I wasn't there a lot, but I knew just from talking to Mom that something was wrong. It was like . . . it was like he just *withdrew* from life. He didn't want to do anything, he wouldn't talk to my mom, he started missing a lot of work, sometimes he wouldn't get out of bed in the mornings . . ."

He paused and shook his head before going on.

"So anyway, by the time I finished my sophomore year, things were pretty bad. I felt really sorry for my mom. I mean Chase was getting into trouble all the time and she was so sick of the way Dad was acting that she was just about ready to leave him . . . it was pretty bad."

"I'm sorry," I said because he glanced at me again and paused. "I didn't know all that."

He nodded and looked away again.

"And then one day," he went on, "Dad just disappeared. No note, no goodbye, no nothing. Considering how he'd been behaving

206

we weren't really all that surprised ... I mean, it had been pretty obvious that something was wrong, but we just kind of figured he was having a mid-life crisis or something. I kept expecting him to come back or at least to call, but he didn't and ... I don't know ... my mom almost seemed relieved. Chase kind of settled down and quit causing problems. Somehow, things actually seemed ... *better* ... with him gone."

He looked at me.

"I know that probably sounds terrible ..."

"No, it doesn't" I answered, shaking my head. "Go on."

"Well, everything's going along pretty good and we were just about used to having Dad gone. I came home for about a week at the end of the summer ..."

He stood up and began pacing back and forth.

"So a day or two before I have to go back to school, Chase comes up to me and he just breaks down. I mean he's sobbing and crying ... he was practically hysterical ... I could hardly understand what he was saying ..."

He stopped pacing and looked at me.

"You can't tell anyone this," he said, looking down at me.

"Okay."

He sat back down and looked at the ground again before he went on.

"My mom had worked it out with Coach Williams to have Chase help the football team out during the summer because she thought it might help keep him out of trouble, but the day my dad disappeared, Chase had told her he wasn't feeling good ... so she'd let him stay home."

"But," I interjected, "Jordan said that Chase and your mom were helping your grandmother paint her house ..."

"No," Tanner said, shaking his head. "That's what Jordan thought, but they were both home."

"But why did Jordan think that then?"

"Chase was really messed up back then . . . getting in trouble all the time and stuff. There's no way my mom was going to let him go to an out-of-state to a baseball camp with Jordan. Plus, I think he actually had a court date that week . . ."

"A *court date?* For what?"

"Oh, who knows," Tanner said. "He was in so much trouble I don't even remember what it was for, but my mom really tried to keep all that from Jordan as much as she could. Jordan wanted Chase to go to baseball camp with him like he always did, but my mom made up some story about how they were going to my grandmother's . . ."

He paused for a long moment.

"So, anyway, that morning, Chase was upstairs sleeping. Mom was at work. Chase heard something that woke him up – he said it sounded like a gunshot. He ran downstairs and didn't find anything. Then he went into the basement . . .

"Chase said that he found my dad dead . . . that he'd shot himself. Chase ran up to him and grabbed the gun and he grabbed at my dad. He was already freaked out and then he realized that his fingerprints were on the gun and he had blood all over himself and he . . . he just panicked."

"What do you mean?"

"I mean he figured he was going to get in trouble . . . that the police were going to think he'd done it. He was already on probation for something and he just . . . he panicked."

"So then what?"

"He spent the rest of the day cleaning everything up and he put my dad's body in the trunk of his car and drove it up to the lake and then he hitched a ride home."

"But the police could have looked at gun powder residue and stuff," I said. "It would have been easy for them to figure out if Chase was telling the truth."

208

"I know," Tanner said, nodding his head. "But he was fifteen years old . . . he didn't really think it through very good."

"But now that your dad's been found, why not just go to the police and tell them the truth?"

"It's too late," Tanner said. "They can't prove anything now . . . all that's going to happen is that everybody'll always question whether Chase did it or not. He doesn't need to spend the rest of his life with everybody wondering if that's what really happened . . ."

"Aren't *you* wondering if that's what really happened?"

Tanner was quiet for a moment.

"I've wondered," he finally admitted. "Do you have any idea what it feels like to wonder if somebody you love could have done something like that?"

He glanced at me.

"Uh . . . yeah," I said, raising an eyebrow at him. "I've got some idea . . ."

He smiled faintly as a knowing look came over his face.

"But I really don't think he did it, David," Tanner said, shaking his head. "I mean, I've known him for his whole life. I know we never really know what somebody else is capable of and I know he's made *a lot* of mistakes, but I really don't think he killed my dad. Maybe one day Chase'll decide to go to the police and tell them what happened, but I just . . . I just don't think that any good's going to come out of *me* doing it.

"Besides that," he went on. "Danica said it sounds like my dad was suffering from depression. She said everything I told her about the way he'd been acting and stuff was consistent with severe depression . . . right down to him committing suicide."

"When did you talk to Danica?"

"I drove up there to see Mike yesterday," he explained.

I wondered briefly if anyone ever went to see poor Mike just for a friendly visit.

"So he knows?"

209

"Yeah," he nodded. "He knows."

"But what if Chase *did* do it, Tanner?"

"On the slim chance that he did," Tanner said in a quiet voice, "Don't you think that God'll take care of it?"

I looked at him for a moment and then nodded.

"But, Tanner?" I said. "Listen. You really need to tell Jordan. He's pretty torn up about this. Can you imagine what he's going through? I mean I really think he needs to know . . ."

"Okay," he finally agreed. "I'll tell him."

We were quiet for a long moment as my mind tried to process everything. I thought about us hitting apples with a baseball bat again, but this time I didn't feel so sad.

"You wanna go in?" I asked. "I'll bet Laci's got a spot all saved for you right next to Natalie."

"She still hasn't given up on that idea, huh?" he smiled at me.

"Nope."

"Then let's go," he said. "I wouldn't want to disappoint Laci."

I counted my talk with Tanner as meaningful conversation number three and didn't worry about having any more for the rest of the night.

~ ~ ~

I'D NEVER SEEN Jordan in such a good mood as when he came over to see me two days later.

"So I gather Tanner talked to you?" I asked, looking at the smile on his face.

"Yeah," he grinned.

"And?" I opened the door so he could step in.

"I talked to Chase too," he nodded, heading toward the couch. "I think he's telling the truth . . . it makes perfect sense . . . and I think I've just about got him convinced to go to the cops and tell them everything . . ."

"So you feel better?"

"I feel great!"

"I'm glad," I said, smiling at him. I picked up Dorito's cap guns off of my chair and sat down.

"All ready for school?" I asked. He was set to fly to Houston in ten days.

"I can't wait!"

"You promised me you'd talk to Charlotte before you left . . ."

His face clouded for just a fraction of a second, but then he nodded.

"Okay," he said. "I will. No problem."

I think he was feeling so happy and relieved about Tanner right then that he would have agreed to just about anything.

~ ~ ~

THE MORNING OF our fourth annual lasagna bake-off, I managed to ring the doorbell even though I was juggling two large paper sacks of groceries. Mrs. White appeared, looked at me and then shook her head.

"Please, help me," I begged. "*Please!?*"

"After you had the nerve to use my mother-in-law's recipe?"

"Oh, come on! That was three years ago. Please?"

She sighed and took one of the bags of groceries from me. I followed her into the kitchen.

"Let's see what you've got," she said, peering into one of the bags. She rifled through both of them and then looked in her cupboard. "If you were going to ask for my help, why didn't you do it *before* you went grocery shopping?"

"What'd I do wrong?"

"Well," she said, "I don't see any sausage."

"I thought you used hamburger."

"You do," she said, "*and* sausage. I didn't see any mushrooms either . . ."

"They're right here." I pulled a can out of one of the bags.

"You've *got* to be kidding me."

"What?"

Twenty minutes later we were at the meat department of the grocery store waiting for the butcher to grind two pounds of sausage and beef together when my phone went off. It was Laci.

"Hi," I said, holding up a finger to my lips so that Mrs. White would stay quiet.

"What are you doing?" she asked.

"Nothing."

"Hi, Laci!" Mrs. White called out toward my phone. I glared at her.

212

"Where are you?" Laci asked.

"Nowhere . . ."

"We're at the grocery store . . ." Mrs. White told her.

"Traitor!" I whispered to her.

"Let's go get some garlic and mushrooms while we're waiting on the meat," Mrs. White said.

I nodded and started following her.

"David!" Laci said.

"What?"

"That's cheating!"

"How's it cheating?" I asked. Mrs. White glanced back at me and smiled. "I'm going to make it all by myself."

"You can't get any help!" Laci said.

"Why not?"

"Because it's *cheating*!"

"Who taught you how to cook?" I asked her.

"My mom . . ."

"Okay, well, *my* mom never taught me how to cook! I don't see how it's cheating just because somebody's teaching me how to cook! How's that any different?"

She didn't say anything so I went on.

"As a matter of *fact*," I said, "I think that *you're* the one who's been cheating since you've had an unfair advantage over me all these years. I think that you should have to forfeit all your wins up to this point."

"I'm still going to beat you, Dave."

"We'll see."

"I love you."

"I love you too."

I snapped my phone shut and smiled at Mrs. White. I was shocked to see tears in her eyes.

"What's wrong?"

"Nothing," she said, shaking her head and trying to smile. I tilted my head at her questioningly and she managed to laugh. "You two are just so good for each other."

"So what's wrong?"

"I was just thinking about Charlotte. I hope she'll be that happy one day."

"Oh," I said, reaching over and rubbing her arm. "She will. I promise she will. She's starting college next week . . . she's going to have a fresh start."

"I'm sure you're right," Mrs. White said, nodding her head. "Now let me show you how to pick out fresh mushrooms. You've got a contest to win."

~ ~ ~

THAT NIGHT, WHEN Tanner arrived, he headed straight for the kitchen where he started loading up a plate.

"Hey, Tanner," I said, walking over to him.

"How's it going?" he asked around a mouthful of cracker and cheese.

"Save room for some of my lasagna," I urged him. "It's going to be *really* good this year."

"I'd rather not," he said, popping a grape into his mouth. "Hey . . . when did Charlotte and Jordan get back together?"

"Huh?"

"Charlotte and Jordan. I saw them on the way over here. When'd they get back together?"

"What makes you think they're back together?"

"Oh," he said, smiling. "*Trust me* . . . they're back together."

"Are you . . . are you sure?"

"Oh yeah," he nodded, smiling even bigger. "I know together when I see together."

Wow . . .

"Wow . . ."

"Have you seen Natalie yet?" he asked.

"Huh?"

"I said have you seen Natalie yet?"

"Ummm . . . no. I'm not even sure if she's coming."

"She's coming," he said, matter-of-factly.

"How do *you* know?" I asked him. I was still so busy trying to wrap my brain around what he'd just said about Charlotte and Jordan that it took me a moment to catch what he was saying now. "And . . . *why do you care?*"

"Because," he smiled. "I know . . . and I care."

"Since *when?*"

215

"Oh," he said, evasively, "for a while . . ."

"Natalie? *Natalie?*"

"Yeah . . . why?"

"Because . . . because Natalie's not your type . . ."

"What makes you say that?" he asked, putting a square of cheese on another cracker and popping it into his mouth.

"Well, for one thing, I happen to know that Natalie wants to get *married* and have kids."

"So?"

"*SO?*" I cried, making the *Pon, Pon* sign at him. "You don't want to 'do the family thing', *REMEMBER?*"

"Who said that?" he asked innocently.

"*YOU DID! YOU SAID THAT!*"

"Naw," he shook his head. "I don't think I ever said that."

"Yes," I argued, "you did."

"Well," he shrugged. "If I said that then maybe I made a mistake."

He leaned down to grab another handful of grapes and then he turned back to face me.

"What's the matter with you, David? Get that look off your face!" He popped two more grapes in his mouth and then he smiled as he chewed. "Hasn't anybody ever told you that sometimes people make mistakes?"

Can just one family make a difference? Can just one person change lives for all eternity? Be sure to read the rest of the books in the *Chop, Chop* series to discover the full impact of Greg and his family in the years that follow.

Book One: *Chop, Chop*
Book Two: *Day-Day*
Book Three: *Pon-Pon*
Book Four: *The Other Brother*
Book Five: *The Other Mothers*
Book Six: *Gone*
Book Seven: *Not Quickly Broken*
Book Eight: *Alone*

On Facebook? Please be sure to become a fan of the *Chop, Chop* page to keep up with the latest!

For more information and free downloadable lesson plans, be sure to visit: www.LNCronk.com

Ordering five or more copies of any of the *Chop, Chop* books? Save 50% off the retail price **and receive free shipping!**

For details, please visit www.LNCronk.com or send an email to: info@LNCronk.com.